TERRITORY

ALWAYS AFTER DARK

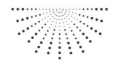

ELLE THORNE

Thank you for reading!

To receive exclusive updates from Elle Thorne and to be the first to
get your hands on the next release,
please sign up for her newsletter.
Put this in your browser:
ellethorne.com/contact

TERRITORY

Trespassing on Tiero territory is begging for trouble.

Shifter Cy's sister is missing. He shouldn't be crossing into Tiero territory to look for her. He should follow proper channels and notify the Tieros, starting with Vax. But Cy can't. He doesn't have the time to wait around for niceties and permissions.
Until he's caught. Damn the luck.

It doesn't help that one of his captors is a beautiful curvy tigress named Lila.

He needs to escape to find his sister, but he hates the thought of leaving the stunning bootilicous tigress behind.

Visit ElleThorne.com to sign up for Elle's newsletter!

ELLE THORNE

CHAPTER ONE

hit. Cy bit back the curse. Shifters had exceptional hearing, and he didn't need to be found, so silence was his motto, silence and stealth, as he crossed through territories without permission. He glanced at the sliver of a moon, casting barely enough light for humans to see, but more than enough for a tiger.

Cyric Villa—Cy to those who knew him really well, which weren't many at all—was out of hunter's block, which was the reason for the word *shit* that he had to bite back and couldn't even let out as a means to release some pressure. He threw the empty block container into a dumpster and stayed close to the alley's wall, his shifter senses on high alert in case anyone out there should be hunting.

They wouldn't be hunting him particularly, since no one should know he was in the area. But shifters patrolled their territory, always on the lookout for trespassing shifters. He felt confident the Tiero would do no less for their territory.

Whether he was ready or not, now that he'd run out of

hunter's block, as soon as the amount he'd just taken wore off, every damned shifter in a not-so-small radius would know he was here. They'd scent him out and hunt him the way dogs did foxes. Images of baying dogs ran through his mind.

Double shit. Running out of block would slow his mission big time because he'd have to be far more cautious and proceed much more slowly. The only thing that would be worse than slowing down would be getting caught. That would bring him to a complete halt.

That didn't bode well for him at all. Or for Petra. Especially not for Petra. The last thing he needed was to be caught. By his estimation, he was now deep in the heart of Tiero territory. He didn't know much about the Tiero tribe; they were too far south of his home for him to stay regularly updated. He'd spent more time avoiding shifters than looking into them or hanging out with them. If he hadn't been a shifter, he'd hunt all of them down. He had a damned good reason to.

As for the Tiero, he'd heard they were decent—not ones to cause trouble and they kept their noses clean. He was Houston-bound, but since the last place his sister had been seen or heard from was Dallas, he had to check Dallas out first. Dallas —Tiero territory. Home of the American branch of the Tiero family.

Cy had heard rumors that made him wonder if Houston was where he'd find his sister. He pushed those rumors out of his mind because they gave rise to images of his sister, dead, mangled, and beaten. He clenched his jaw. He'd seen dead and mangled loved ones already. He had no interest in seeing that again.

His tiger growled a warning signal in Cy's mind. Alarmed, concerned, and unwilling to be caught off-guard, he shifted into his tiger with an expedient and silent rush of adrenaline. He was close to his tiger. They were like two in the same skin. He knew some shifters didn't do so well with theirs, but Cy had never had a problem, not since he was eighteen and he'd shifted so his tiger could help him save Petra's life. His tiger was more than Cy's alter ego. He was his best friend.

He leapt, taking them onto a low rooftop. He ran across that one and leapt to a taller building. For more than an hour, Cy traveled rooftop to rooftop across the Dallas Metroplex, scenting and listening, hunting for any sign of Petra.

Something. There should have been something here. Petra had called him from Dallas on the day she was supposed to return home. There should be a sign of her. He was close to the hotel her group had been in. Surely there should be something near here.

Thirty minutes later, after canvassing an even wider perimeter, he saw the large red lettering announcing the hotel she'd stayed at a city block away.

He leapt from one building to the next then padded across scaffolding.

He was brought up short when his tiger froze then snarled.

Cy paused, scented, listened, and looked about him. Going from one edge of the roof to another, he scanned the streets and buildings below. What had his tiger sensed? What was causing his alarms to go off and the fur on the back of his neck to stand up? He snarled.

Shifters. He scented shifters. He inhaled deeply, his tiger nostrils flaring. *Damn.* Cy surveyed escape routes. He could head in the other direction then double back to see if he could find Petra's scent.

He slipped behind a large air conditioning unit then

hunched low in the shadows. He scented again, trying to isolate and count the number of shifters he could find. He counted at least a half dozen. *All males. All tigers. What the hell?* Was he near Tiero headquarters? Why such a strong concentration of shifter scents in one area?

He crouched lower. So many shifters, and he'd be willing to bet none of them would be friendly. Why would they be? It wasn't like he'd asked if he could cross into their territory. It wasn't like he'd told them he was a friendly. Why should they trust him? For all they knew, he meant them harm.

He definitely needed to slip away, unseen and unheeded, and return when the area was a little less congested with shifters.

He rose from his hiding place behind the massive air conditioning unit.

Fuck!

He dropped back down. *Oh, hell.* They were on the rooftop with him. He was surrounded, and there were at least eight of them. All tigers. All large, and they carried themselves with a predatory military bearing.

He calmed his pulse, hoping they wouldn't pick up the heartbeat of someone who had adrenaline rushing through his system with the force of a rocket booster.

He needed a plan, quick, and it needed to be a good one. Yeah, fat chance of that on such short notice. His instinct was to fight them off, but he was a realist. The odds were against his coming out of this alive. He threw something together in his mind and prayed there'd be an opening when he got to the other side of the roof. All he needed was one solid opening between the shifters and he could leap to the same roof he'd just come from.

4

His muscles tight, his legs ready, he sprang from behind the AC unit, leapt over the first shifter, his hind feet skimming the shifter's head, then he pounced to the concrete, sprinted two quick strides and leapt again.

Except Cy hadn't counted on the largest tiger he'd ever seen—almost as large as Cy—appearing out of nowhere and striking him midair, knocking him to the concrete with a force that shot the air out of his lungs.

Cy didn't stay on the concrete long. Remaining in his tiger form, he jumped up and bared his teeth at the other shifters.

His options to leave unscathed and without hurting anyone had been taken away.

Only one plan remained.

Fight.

CHAPTER TWO

L ila slipped out of Sanctuary, the tiger enclosure housing an assortment of tigers on view for club patrons. The thing the patrons didn't know was all the tigers were shifters.

Sanctuary, a glass and metal bar enclosure, took up the whole forty-third floor of Tiero Tower One—one of two side-by-side high rises owned by Lila's family, the Tieros. Five glass-covered walkways connected the buildings, allowing occupants to travel from building to building without venturing outside. The Tiero Towers ranked amongst the most extravagant and coveted buildings in Dallas. Partiers from far and wide made After Dark a must-see on their visits to the Dallas Metroplex.

She headed toward the door to After Dark, tugging on her green evening dress, smoothing wrinkles out. Whenever she shifted into her tigress skin then shifted back, her clothing was always a bit askew, as if she'd been getting it on in the backseat of someone's car. She'd slip into the dressing room to make sure she didn't look too rumpled.

I should be thankful. What if she ripped through her clothing and was naked when she shifted back into her human form? *Okay, yeah, that would suck. Completely.*

Almost nine. Almost opening time. She'd make it just in time for Veila to run the staff meeting. Vax normally ran the meetings, but he was in New Orleans with Callie. A smile drifted across Lila's face as she thought of how happy her half-brother was now that he had Callie as a mate. Not that he was ever sour; he'd just had a habit of brooding and keeping to himself.

Lila shrugged. It wasn't like women didn't like brooding, but Vax had been impervious to women—until Callie, a curvy human grad student, had come along. He'd fallen head over heels for her, and he'd risked infuriating the Tiero tribe. He'd broken the code, had taken her—a human—as a mate, and now he was out of town.

When word got back to their father and some of the elders in the tribe, she knew there'd be a flight or two headed toward the Dallas-Fort Worth Airport. The elders would have the Tiero Towers as their destination, and Vax's ass as their target.

Vax was braced to do battle. He'd couple-bonded and marked Callie as his, and he'd defend that to the death. Or to his resignation. Whichever the elders thought was needed.

If there was a battle, Lila knew Veila would side with her brother. That was to be expected; they were full brother and sister. Lila and Sophie were Vax and Veila's half-sisters and would be expected to side with their father.

I'd better ask Sophie how she feels about this. Lila was much more inclined to side with Vax. The Tiero Code that denied shifters the right to mate with humans was archaic, and she had no idea what premise it had been based on, anyway.

Her phone vibrated on her hip. She detached it.

Veila.

Lila engaged the call with a quick tap on the screen. "Hey, I'll be there in a second. You ready for the meeting already? I thought I had a few minutes."

"No. Something's come up. Gavin called."

Gavin, Lila's ex. An ex who hadn't lasted long, but she had to see him practically every day, since he was the head of Tiero security.

Veila's tone made something in Lila's stomach tighten and turn like a winch.

"I need you to do something," Veila continued.

Lila wondered what it was. Had a hostess not shown up? Or a waitress? "No problem. Go ahead."

"Gavin said there's a stray shifter in our territory. He wasn't too far from Tiero Towers."

"Okayyyy." *So what's that mean to me?* Lila waited for Veila to tell her what she needed from her.

"With Vax out of town, I don't want to leave After Dark. Can you take care of it?"

"Sure." Well, it would be nice to get out of the club for a change. The idea of doing something totally different was cool. Though the idea of seeing Gavin didn't really thrill Lila too much.

"He's at the warehouse next to the recycling center."

"I'll go right now." Lila looked down at her evening gown. She wasn't exactly dressed for that part of town, but what the hell.

"Call Gavin for the deets."

Hell no, she wasn't going to call Gavin. She and Gavin barely got along. "I'll take care of it." Lila ended the call without actually agreeing to call Gavin. She wasn't going to. Period.

CHAPTER THREE

Cy groaned. He was in his human skin, and he was pretty sure he had a few broken ribs and some internal injuries. He tried to take a deep breath, but it felt like the world's largest boa constrictor was wrapped around his upper body and squeezing the life out of him.

He opened his eyes a tiny bit, just a slit, knowing he wouldn't like what he saw. He was right. Damn, was he ever. Large rods of metal all around him affirmed he was in a cage.

He was in a fucking cage. Like an animal. Rage raced through his body, and his tiger yearned to get out and inflict some serious damage. But what could either he or his tiger do against metal? Nothing. Not a damned thing.

He kept his eyes semi-closed while he tried to survey the area.

"Hey," said a voice he didn't recognize.

Cy strained to hear. Whoever spoke was definitely a shifter, and whoever it was not in the room. Cy listened for heartbeats nearby. None, unless they could fool him. He didn't think they could.

He turned his head slightly, and almost grunted out loud from the pain in his neck and back. He needed time, so his shifter healing could happen. Except time wasn't something he—or Petra—had the luxury of. He looked in the direction he'd turned.

No one there.

He turned the other way.

No one there, either.

He studied his surroundings. He was alone in an empty warehouse save for a few crates in one corner and some large, tarp-covered items in another.

"Gavin." It was the same voice that had just spoken. "Is Vax on his way out?" The voice came from outside the warehouse, but not very far.

"No. I called Veila. She's handling it."

The one who had answered must be Gavin, though the name didn't mean anything to Cy. He didn't think the guy was a Tiero. Though, to be honest, he really didn't know all the Tieros. He hadn't bothered to learn their names. Why would he? He avoided shifters as a rule, and he'd never expected to be this far south, in their territory. He did know "Vax" was Vittorio Tiero, alpha of this territory.

Cy was in a cage in Tiero territory and had no way to find Petra and no way to help her.

A couple of shuffling noises, some footsteps, and the shifters were walking into the warehouse, heading for the cage Cy was in. *Six of them. Great. Not so easy to outnumber.* Where were the rest of the ones who had joined in his ass-kicking before they'd locked him up? Probably outside, as rein-forcements.

The biggest shifter of all, the one who had intercepted Cy's leap, stepped closest. "About time you woke up. Why are you in Tiero territory?"

Cy recognized his voice. He was the one the other shifter had called Gavin.

Cy didn't answer, staring at the tall man with the broad shoulders.

"This can go down easy or hard. It's up to you. We'll get answers, or you'll be dead. What's your name?" Gavin crossed his arms over his chest, eyes narrowed.

Cy strained to sit up, keeping a grunt of pain buried deep in his chest. He sat, propped up against the cage, using the bars to keep himself from falling over. Once he was in a seated position, breathing was a bit more difficult, but at least he didn't feel like a helpless victim, lying on the cage floor.

One of the other shifters stepped forward. "He's not answering," he told Gavin.

"Put a little bit of hurt on him," Gavin said, and turned his back.

Three shifters, then a fourth, joined each other in front of his cage. Using the bars to pull himself to a stand, Cy rose, all six feet seven inches of him.

He didn't care how hurt he was, he wasn't going down easy, he wasn't going down alone, and if he could just get an edge... just a little edge... he'd slip out of the cage and the warehouse and head south for Houston.

One of the shifters unlocked the cage. Cy walked to the other side. Maybe "walked" was the wrong word; with the pain he was in, he did a zombie shuffle to the other side.

All four came in. Tiger shifters, none of them under six foot. The tallest maybe six four. They squared their shoulders, but he sensed the tension in their bodies. He'd inflicted some pain on them, and they weren't eager for more.

Bring it. He glared at them, angry at the disruption of his mission.

Cy's hackles rose. His sensors flipped out. Another heartbeat approached, but...

Something was different about this one.

CHAPTER FOUR

Lila pulled into the parking lot. Yes, this was the warehouse. She recognized the Tiero SUV with its dark-tinted windows. Gavin's SUV. A sour note struck her stomach.

Here we go. She got out and shut car the door as quietly as possible, hoping to gain a bit of an advantage on Gavin. She wished they could stop being so adversarial. It was time for him to get over it already. *Maybe I contribute to it, too,* she had to admit to herself.

Two of Gavin's men stood partially hidden in the shadows near the SUV. They jumped to attention when she walked toward them.

"Lila. Hi, what—"

She held up a finger, putting it to her lips. Then she pointed to the door, warning them to be silent and letting them know she was going in without an argument from them.

They nodded. They knew who was boss.

She slipped through the open door, and the first thing she saw was a large cage, large as a railroad car. There were several shifters inside, and Gavin and one of his men were outside. The door was shut.

The shifters inside were scuffling, fists were flying. Grunts of pain filled the air. She knew most of them; they were Gavin's men. One she didn't recognize was throwing punches, but, unfortunately, it seemed for every one he threw, he caught two or three, and in very painful-looking areas.

The shifter she didn't recognize stopped and stared toward her, as if he knew her—recognized her. Gavin's men paused for a second, as if confused that he'd stopped fighting. Then they went at him again, even though he was motionless, his eyes glued on her.

Gavin's men were pummeling the stranger. Blow after blow struck his solid body, that wide chest, bare because his shirt was in shreds. She fought back a gasp when she noticed the wounds from claws and canines marring his body. *What the hell did Gavin's men do to him?*

She walked to Gavin, stood next to him. He didn't acknowledge her presence. He knew she was there, and yet he had to play this stupid game.

Fine.

In the background, the sounds of fists striking flesh were relentless.

"Tell them to stop." She kept her voice level and her temper under control.

He didn't look at her, didn't tell his men anything.

She walked in front of Gavin and planted her high heels shoulder-width apart, facing him. She wasn't a short woman, but even in heels she was still a few inches shorter than he was.

"Now." She put her index finger on his chest, pressing on muscle that had no give.

He clenched his jaw, the muscles working in his chiseled, handsome face. "Stop."

He gritted the word out as if he were biting on a bullet. He didn't say it loudly because he didn't have to. His team's shifter hearing picked it up.

Gavin's men froze. The stranger was still staring at Lila, still unmoving. Gavin's team turned to look at him then their eyes fell on Lila.

Lila and Gavin's history was no mystery to any of them. They knew the fireworks that had flown between them.

She glared at them. She was pissed Gavin dared to defy her. This was not the way to show allegiance or respect for her position.

She snapped her fingers and nodded for his men to leave the cage. The one nearest the cage's door turned away from the stranger and took a step toward it, unlatched it, and moved out. Single file, each of Gavin's men followed then one of them latched the door behind him, turning the thick key once. A loud click confirmed the door was locked. They walked toward Lila and Gavin.

She held her hand out, expecting the key. Lucky for the man holding it, he didn't look at Gavin. As pissed as she was, she'd have shifted and gone for Gavin's jugular, knowing he wouldn't do anything to defend himself because of her position.

Passing Lila and Gavin silently, Gavin's men lined up and

waited by the warehouse exit. She glanced at the stranger, finally able to get a full, unobstructed view of him.

Lila tried to look at him objectively, but there was a huge problem. Her tigress had leapt to full attention and focused on the man with an intensity that almost scared her. No, her tigress wasn't focused on the man; her tigress was fully engrossed in his tiger. It was as if the man and Lila had both ceased to exist, leaving two tigers and an emotion burning between them with a fierceness that was almost tangible.

Lila pushed her tigress aside and could tell from her tigress's reaction the man was trying to do the same with his tiger, but he wasn't having anywhere near the same amount of success Lila had at harnessing her tigress.

What the hell is this about? She'd never seen her tigress act like this. With her tigress's flare-up under control, Lila took the chance to scrutinize the stranger.

God, he was huge. Taller than Gavin by a bit, she'd guess, and Gavin wasn't short. His eyes were dark. How dark? She'd have to see them up close to find out. His hair would have reached his collar, if he'd had a shirt on. Black, wavy, thick. She swallowed a lump as she scanned his shoulders and chest. The man was built.

Next to her, Gavin cleared his throat. She fought to keep her pulse under control but was pretty sure Gavin had already picked up on the way her tigress had reacted to the stranger. Damn him. Gavin knew her way too well.

"Who is he?" She turned toward Gavin, her voice husky, though she didn't want it to be. She cursed her tigress for her attraction to the stranger's tiger.

"An interloper." Gavin's words were cut from ice.

"Obviously." She didn't hide the sarcasm in her remark. "Other than that?" She bit back a remark her tigress was ready to spit out—Gavin's security skills were lacking if he didn't know who this stranger was who'd managed to reach their territory. Then she was glad she hadn't said it. She'd already hurt Gavin enough, judging by the way he still reacted around her. Plus, his job wasn't to keep shifters from crossing their boundaries; no one could really do that. His job was to be sure no Tiero came to harm, and none had on his watch.

"He's not talking." Gavin crossed his arms over his chest. "That's what we were trying to rectify when you interrupted."

"Not even his name?" Lila looked back at the man who still hadn't taken his eyes off her.

"Not even that." Gavin exhaled. "Yet."

The stranger shifted his weight, as if he were in discomfort. That's when Lila picked up on his signal, one she was certain he didn't want to transmit. Maybe his tiger had let it slip. The man was wounded. Seriously.

"Leave us." She turned back to Gavin.

A tiny shake of his head let her know he didn't want to agree.

"Now." Then she gave him a consolation. "If you wish, you can wait outside."

"What if he's a rover? Or one of those who attacked Kane."

Lila frowned. "What are you talking about? You mean the shifter who saved Sophie when she was attacked?" Why did she feel so out of touch? Why did Gavin seem to know more than she did?

Gavin nodded, which was just his way of not answering directly. He knew more than he was letting on. Did Vax's absence for a few days have anything to do with it?

"Leave us."

Gavin hesitated.

"Now."

"I'm supposed to take care of you in Vax's absence."

"I'm not a child. I don't need taking care of."

CHAPTER FIVE

C y watched the blonde with hips he'd—
Jesus.

Why was he thinking like this? Here he was, his ass beat to a pulp, his body begging for mercy, and all he could think about was the scent and taste of this woman. Okay, he couldn't take all the credit. His tiger was in a mode Cy had never seen him in before.

Wanting her. Needing her. Seeking to bond with her, with a single-mindedness that was alarming, confusing, and premature. This was way too premature. He barely knew her.

The blonde walked his way, those hips swaying, her hourglass figure encased in a green evening dress that sparkled with every step she took, catching the dim lighting and reflecting tiny bits of light. Her hair reached halfway down her back and moved with every step. He liked her attitude. This was a woman he'd like to know better. In his chest, his tiger rumbled agreement.

She stopped in front of the door. Emotion flowed through

Cy and his tiger. She was stunning. Her eyes were an emerald green that picked up the dress's sparkle. She tapped her finger on her lip, and of course Cy couldn't concentrate on anything but those full pink lips.

Without saying a word, she kept those mesmerizing eyes glued on him while she assessed him, vivid green lasers traveling up and down his body as she surveyed him.

"You're hurt."

Jesus. Her voice was like honey being poured into his mouth. He swallowed down the lump she left in his throat and hoped she didn't notice the one she'd raised in his pants. "I'm fine. I need to go."

"That's a bit complicated," she said. "There are questions."

"I'm not answering them. What makes you think no one can hear our conversation right now?"

"True." She nodded. "Sync? I'm coming in."

He was taken aback. "Aren't you afraid of me?"

"No, but if you did succeed in killing me, you wouldn't live one moment after Gavin found my dead body."

"Fair enough. I wouldn't do that anyway."

"I know."

She unlocked the door and stepped inside the cage with him. He was stunned. What made her think she could trust him? She closed the door behind them then took the key out of the lock and tucked it into her bra. He shifted immediately.

She shifted, too. She was a beautiful white tigress, majestic and queenly.

More beautiful as a tigress than as a human, his tiger rumbled.

Not a chance, Cy argued. *She's more stunning as a human.*

21

His tiger snarled. *Look at those curves. She wouldn't have curves like that if she wasn't a tigress.*

Lila and her tigress stalked around him, a wide circle, her green eyes dark and inquisitive. Why *are you here? Why are you in Tiero territory, unannounced and uninvited?*

First, your name, tigress. What is it? He couldn't imagine not knowing the name of the woman he would make his mate. Yes, he'd decided, and there was no doubt in his tiger's mind either.

Lila Tiero.

Ah, one of the Tiero. He nodded his appreciation for her honesty. Lila. He liked her name as much as he liked—craved—needed—wanted her.

You haven't told me yours.

He made a wide circle around her, assessing. He wasn't ready to discuss his name, so he answered her other question. *My sister came down with a group of interns for a job interview. The others returned. She did not.*

Lila gave a quick snarl, maybe in acknowledgment he hadn't answered her question. *What makes you think she's in Tiero territory?*

It's the last place she called me from. Dallas.

Foolish of you to come here like this, during a time when we have heightened security. We've had issues with our boundaries being infringed upon.

You are not Vax Tiero. He stated the obvious.

No, that's my big brother.

So little sisters now answer for alphas? His tiger growled. Cy was anxious to go and answering questions wouldn't help him get out of here any quicker.

She bristled visibly at the insult she clearly perceived. Instantly, he regretted it.

So you don't think I'm capable? Is that it?

Please accept my apologies. My tiger interferes with my thoughts. He shouldn't have.

So that is the way your tiger feels? I would guess you're unmated and likely to stay that way.

A part of Cy wanted to laugh at the way she and her tigress had put him and his tiger back in their place, completely taking them down a notch. The other part of him remembered he was his tiger, and they were one.

You didn't want to contact the authorities to look for your sister?

He gave her a look of disdain and cocked his head. *That would be pure foolishness. Shifter business stays in the shifter world. I don't want humans involved in this. I'd think a Tiero would understand that better than anyone, considering how proud the Tiero are of shifter codes in general and their own codes, specifically.*

That code is history. She stood taller, proud of what she was saying. *Why are you, her brother, here seeking her, instead of her father?*

We have no father or mother. I am the closest thing my baby sister has to a father.

You can't just roam in and out of territories at will. You could be confused for a rover or a subversive on an assignment, or an enemy looking to increase your territory.

You're right. Please, release me so I can find my sister.

CHAPTER SIX

The stranger was a beautiful, vivid, orange and black Siberian. The most beautiful that Lila had ever laid eyes on.

He was massive. Deep within her, Lila's tigress was purring and practically preening. She wanted to caution her tigress to contain her emotions. To contain herself, but a part of Lila was just as attracted to the man as her tigress was to the Siberian. Lila wanted him, and she didn't even know the name of the man she'd be willing to—

Why the hell was she thinking this way? This wasn't like her. She shook her tigress head to clear it and to stop her tigress from influencing her, though Lila knew it wasn't the tigress alone.

Your name? She would give him another chance to answer.

Cyric Villa. My friends call me Cy.

I'd like to call you Cy. Oh for fuck's sake. Where did that come from? She cursed at herself and her tigress. Flirting? When the man was here looking for his sister? The best thing she could do for him was help him find Petra, who had prob-ably run off with a new boyfriend or something.

Get over yourself and these damned bonding and mating hormones she told her tigress—and herself.

HE COULDN'T BELIEVE SHE WANTED TO CALL HIM CY. IT WAS almost as if she was flirting with him then, the next moment, she looked angry. Damn, this woman was confusing.

You're not telling me everything. Lila's eyes narrowed. *What are you holding back?*

He paced back and forth in the cage. *There are rumors of a production.*

Be more specific. She sat on her haunches, her neck long and elegant, her muscles sleek, her body lush, a tigress in her prime, just as she was in her human skin.

Cy stopped pacing and faced her. His inner voice was taut as he fought to keep his fierceness out of his tiger's sync voice. *Fights. Between shifters. Sometimes men, sometimes women. They drug them up and have them fight. Some of the opponents are genetically enhanced shifters.*

She snorted and made a snuffling sound. *That's unbeliev-able. The most incredible spinning of a story I've ever heard.*

I'm telling you what I heard. There's an organized fighting ring, to the death, between shifters and sometimes against enhanced shifters.

Who puts these on? Who watches them? Disbelief colored her tigress's sync voice. *Enhanced? What's that mean?*

A shifter puts them on, that's what I've heard. Both humans and shifters watch. That's all I heard. Enhanced, whatever that means. He wondered if it meant those shifters had special abilities, or if they were genetically enhanced. How the hell would that even happen?

Lila's posture became defensive. *Not in this territory. Vax wouldn't allow or support anything like that. What's your sister's name?*

Then in a nearby territory. I'm sure of it. Her name is Petra. Now let me out.

No. I'll look into it. Trust me. Please. She shut the sync down.

She shifted, dug the key out of her pocket, unlocked the door, and left.

Cy couldn't hurt her, and he didn't stop her. He had to trust her, even though he was working on another plan.

CHAPTER SEVEN

"Not in this territory," Lila had told Cy, and that was the truth. If it was happening, Vax would have found out and put a stop to it, and she would have heard about it. Vax would have brought it up at one of their meetings.

She needed a plan. She paused, leaning against the warehouse wall near the exit. She stared at the shifter, watching him turn from that beautiful Siberian tiger into a really gorgeous man.

She stood in the shadows, and yet his eyes stayed glued on her, watching her from behind the bars. Why did she have to meet him under circumstances like this? She'd love to have a chance to get to know him better, to get to know his tiger better.

She shook her head, took out her cell phone and dialed Veila so she could talk to her. No, she couldn't do that. Gavin was just outside, or at least one of his men was. She could hear the heartbeat. They'd tell Gavin whatever she said. She didn't need any interference. She hung up quickly.

Texting was better. No one could listen in, and that way, no one could ask a bunch of questions—that someone being Veila.

She texted Veila that she was looking into the shifter matter and would contact her later.

Lila pressed send and looked at the man named Cy. She'd help him. She believed him. The only problem was she couldn't let him go. Doing so would be foolish and could actually get him hurt. Gavin would come after him because Cy was trespassing and, in Gavin's eyes, could be a threat.

Yes, the safest place for Cy was in a cage right now.

His tiger's heartbeat was strong, beating a rhythm that called to hers. Why did she have to meet him like this? Urgency to save his sister and to keep this giant of a shifter from the pain of burying a loved one fueled her adrenaline with a need to act.

With one final glance at the Siberian shifter and a rumble of protest from her tigress for leaving him behind, Lila slipped out the exit and into the darkness of the night.

Gavin and his men were still there, standing by the SUV. She approached Gavin but didn't say a word.

He took her cue. "Leave us," he said to his men.

Lila stood up as tall as she could and stared him in the eye. "I'm going to look into something."

"What did he tell you?" Gavin's eyes narrowed; clearly, he didn't trust Cy. "Did he tell you his name? Who he is? What he wants?"

She nodded, turning. She didn't owe Gavin an explanation.

He put his hand on her arm. "You can't go alone. Vax wouldn't want that."

She looked at his hand pointedly. "That's not your place to say." She was tired of Gavin always being overprotective.

He took his hand off her arm. "I'm going to Vax for approval."

"You're not to bother my brother. He needs some time with his mate." *And I need to figure out what the hell is going on here while I get a little bit of distance from that sexy Siberian because his presence is way too distracting.*

She kept the key to the cage in her safekeeping. She didn't want Gavin to be able to get to Cy... and she didn't need Cy following her or interfering.

CHAPTER EIGHT

L ila's figure was a glorious hourglass silhouette as she walked away from him. Her ass was a round shelf bringing to his mind visions of cold nights, warm fires, and log cabins. He shook his head to clear it, or to clear his tiger's.

She had almost made it to the warehouse exit when she paused and turned to the left, showing him a different silhouette—lovely full breasts, her stomach, and thighs—round, and made for pleasure. She swiveled and leaned against the wall. Then she didn't move. In the dimness, he could see and feel her emerald gaze intent on him.

Cy kept his eyes on her while she leaned against the warehouse wall. Surely, she knew he could see her. She was a shifter; she knew their capabilities. Yet she just stood there, watching him. Her breathing ranged from normal to escalated, as though adrenaline began to pump throughout her body.

His tiger reached out to her tigress, letting her hear his heartbeat, listening for hers.

After a few moments, she reached for her phone. It looked like she sent a text or an email, then she squared her shoulders as if preparing for battle and went outside.

With his tiger hearing, he overheard Lila tell Gavin she was going to look into this on her own.

Had she lost her mind? What made her think she wouldn't be in danger? If they'd kidnapped his sister to put her into the illegal shows, they'd do the same to Lila. Now he'd have to worry about saving two females.

Christ. What the hell was she thinking?

His tiger seethed, grunting and growling, not giving Cy a moment to think. He couldn't concentrate on coming up with a plan because of the noise his tiger was making in his head.

Gavin and eight other shifters entered the warehouse. They walked in formation, as if they were part of an elite, highly synchronized dance team. *Or a military team.* Yes, that was exactly what they were, a highly effective, well-trained military team. He hoped the close quarters of the cage would work to his advantage. It could only fit a few of them and even then, they wouldn't be able to move about very much.

Gavin's jaw had a set to it that didn't make Cy think he planned on having a friendly conversation. Cy took a deep breath. He didn't plan to die, although he wasn't sure if that was Gavin's intention.

The shifters stopped in front of the cage. Gavin brought up the rear.

One of his men turned to Gavin. "The key?"

CHAPTER NINE

L ila pulled out of the warehouse lot, spinning her tires on the loose gravel, mostly because she was in a hurry to get the hell out of there before Gavin tried to stop her. Or before he asked her for the key.

"Now what, smarty-pants?" she muttered to herself, because she didn't have a clue where to go to find out if there was an underground fight club for shifters. If she couldn't figure it out in Dallas, her own stomping grounds, she was screwed, because she certainly wouldn't be able to learn anything about it in a whole different area, like Houston.

The Tieros had no relationship to speak of with the shifters who held control over the Houston territory, a group of Germans called Nielsen. All of them were wolves. None of them had a relationship with the Tiero family. Sure, okay, the Tiero hadn't been on the continent as long as some of the other shifter tribes, but still, you'd think they'd want to have a relationship of some sort. She scoffed at the silliness of all the territory rules shifters had.

Then again, she thought of Sophie almost being kidnapped and wondered if the whole territories and boundaries thing wasn't good, after all.

"Oh, shit!" It hit her like a brick tossed out of a second-story window. What about Sophie's close call when some shifters had been trying to kidnap her? Could that be the same group?

Rovers could be hired to do whatever. *Hmmmm.* She wondered if the rovers were being paid to get "contestants" to fight.

She grabbed her phone and called Sophie.

The phone rang four times before she answered.

"Took you long enough," she told her younger sister. Then she quickly pulled the phone away from her ear. The sound of music blaring at After Dark was loud as hell.

"What?" Sophie yelled.

"Go somewhere quiet," she yelled back.

"Okay."

The music faded. A moment later, all that was left was the dull thump of bass.

"You know I'm working, right?" Sophie sounded perplexed.

"Yeah, I'm sorry. This is important. When you... when those rovers tried to kidnap you, when Kane saved you... Where were you, exactly?"

"What? You called me for th—"

"It's important. If it wasn't, I wouldn't have. Seriously. I need to know."

Sophie huffed a sigh at the other end. "I hope you're not getting into any trouble."

"Come on, Soph, it's me, remember? You know I don't do trouble."

"Okay. Well, it was after the after-hours club. You and Veila went to breakfast, remember? Well, I met this guy. He was nice, funny, and a shifter, of course."

Of course. Lila didn't say it out loud.

"Anyway," Sophie continued. "We went walking—"

"What? In that part of— What the hell were you—" Lila bit back the rest of her response. She would talk to Sophie about her naiveté later. Right now, she needed information. "Sorry. Keep talking."

"I know, okay?" Sophie really did sound like she'd learned her lesson. "Anyway, so we went walking south, past the old restaurant auction place, you know?"

"Yeah, I know where that is."

"Near there, in front of the car shop where Vax had the stereo put in his Porsche? The guy said there was a party across the street, except there was no party. There were some guys there, and then he vanished, and they tried to kidnap me. Then that bear, Kane, came out. Well, that's it."

"Have you given Vax the details?"

"Hell, no. Not all of them, and you'd better not either, or I'll never tell you anything again."

"Okay, okay. I promise."

"Now I've got to go back to work before Veila thinks I'm slacking. What else?"

"That's it. Thanks, sis. Love you." Lila pressed End.

That gave her a starting point. Something was better than nothing.

CHAPTER TEN

G avin shook his head. "That wasn't the only key." He reached into his pocket and pulled one out.

Cy fought the smile wanting to come out at his good luck. In fact, he wanted to cheer. A key was the only way Cy could get out of here and go find Lila and Petra. He was going to give that Lila a sound spanking when he found her for locking him in.

Of course, his cock twitched at the idea of planting his palm on her round ass.

Great. Not what he needed to think of at a time when he was going to have to outman, outfight, and outrun eight powerful shifters.

Leaning against the bars, his head down somewhat, but still watching from beneath his lowered lids as the shifters approached and assessed them. He determined which of them were weak, which were right-handed or left-handed, and which were injured. He scanned their clothing for weapons and wasn't surprised most of them were unarmed.

Gavin clicked his teeth, a sound of disgust or humor, Cy wasn't sure. Cy studied the other shifter.

"So, you told her something about yourself? I suppose you shifted and synced?"

Cy didn't answer him.

"I already know beating the hell out of you doesn't yield any answers. So why did you tell her? What did you tell her?" Gavin cocked his head, waiting.

Cy remained silent.

"You do realize she's headstrong." Gavin shook his head then looked at his men.

Then it hit Cy—the shifter was in love with Lila. He was worried about her, just as Cy was worried about her.

Finally, Cy spoke. "You have history with her?"

Gavin's head snapped toward him. "Why do you care?"

He could tell from the way Gavin's pulse reacted he'd gotten it right. Gavin and Lila had history. The question was, was it just history, or did they have something going on now? He wanted to think they didn't; otherwise, she wouldn't have reacted to him the way she had, nor would her tigress. He shrugged. It was none of Gavin's business Cy wanted Lila or the degree to which he wanted her. That was between Lila and him.

"So, it looks like I have very limited options. Kill you. However, if I kill you and anything happens to Lila, it will be on my conscience that I could have done something differently. Another option is to see if we really can't break you and get answers." Gavin shook his head. "No, I don't think that'll work. Maybe I'll just leave you here and see if our best scenter can't find her."

"You'll be risking her life." Cy's voice was grave. "Let me go. I'll look for her."

"Why would you give a damn about her? You just met her."

Cy locked eyes with the shifter. He seemed to be an honorable man, and the Tiero had a good reputation. He was counting on that. "I think, deep down, you know I will."

Gavin looked at his men then back at Cy. "We'll tail you."

"No. You'll bring too much attention to me. Do you have any spare hunter's block?"

"So we can't find you?" Gavin laughed. "Can you believe this guy?"

"You're wasting time," he reminded him, clenching his jaw. Time that could be valuable to Petra and Lila. "And she's going to be talking to dangerous people."

"We're going with you. Take it or leave it." Gavin's tone held finality.

We'll see.

CHAPTER ELEVEN

F orty-five minutes later, with her cell phone battery almost dead from using maps to find the damned place, and without her charger, a frustrated Lila pulled onto the street with the store where Vax had taken his car to get a stereo installed.

Store, she scoffed inwardly. *Hardly*. She didn't remember this street looking quite so sinister when Vax had brought the Porsche here. Then again, it had been broad daylight.

She glanced at the empty building across the street. This was the right place, she was sure of it. She drove past slowly, not wanting to attract attention by just pulling in. The street was completely empty. No vehicles. No people.

Still, this was the place, and, based on what Sophie had said, Lila had to look into it.

She drove a block farther, parked her Honda behind a convenience store, and got out. She took a step.

Click.

Then two more steps.

Click, click.

She looked down at her heels. *Sheesh.* She couldn't sneak up on anyone like this. Why not just use an announcement service to proclaim her arrival? She tiptoed around the corner, slipped behind the dumpster, and shifted.

Much better. She looked down at her paws. She wouldn't be heard coming now.

One leap took her over the wood fence behind the convenience store. A few more leaps and several bounds, and a couple of moments of loping, and she was scaling the buildings, well on her way to her destination. One final leap and Lila landed on top of the building where Sophie had said her attempted abduction took place.

She halted, taking a second to scent. Nothing. Then again, if the shifters were using block, like Vax always did, she wouldn't be able to smell them, would she? She smiled inwardly at Vax and the amount of block he used to try to hide how he felt when he was around Callie. There wasn't enough block in the world to cover that scent completely. That's how much her big brother was into the curvy brunette. She sobered up for a moment, hoping one day she'd find someone as devoted to her as Vax was to Callie.

An image of Cy's face crossed her mind. She pushed it away. She needed to concentrate on business right now.

Lila couldn't scent anyone. She listened for heartbeats but came up empty. Still, she had faith she was in the right place. She ran to the back of the building and leapt off the shambling rooftop to the ground. After shifting back into her human skin, she tiptoed to the back door.

Locked.

After a moment of rummaging through a pile of junk as

quietly as she could, she picked up a flat metal bar and shoved it between the jamb and the door. Pushing all her weight behind it, she shoved once, then twice. The third time did it. The door popped, the lock giving, some of the jamb shedding wood.

With a quick glance and a listen to verify she was still alone and hadn't attracted attention, Lila opened the door just enough to slip inside then pulled it closed behind her.

She looked at the bar still in her hands. *What the hell? Might as well keep it; it'll make a good weapon.* A part of her hoped she wouldn't need a weapon, but another part of her hoped she would because if she didn't, that would mean she'd been completely on the wrong track.

She blew out an exasperated breath.

She sniffed.

There it was!

The faint scent of shifters. It wasn't a fresh scent. She tried to identify the shifters, but the smell wasn't clear. Then again, scenting wasn't really her strongest shifter attribute. Nonetheless, there'd been shifters here, so she felt a bit better about her chances of learning something—sometime.

Now it was all about the waiting and finding the best place to wait. She surveyed the dark warehouse. Barrels lined up along one wall. Extra-large wooden boxes lined up against the other wall. The concrete floor was covered with debris scattered and strewn all over. It looked like the scene from a fight. Maybe that's what it was. A remnant from Sophie's close call?

She slipped behind the large boxes, finding a perfect little cubby that would hide her. Times like this she wished she had some block. Oh well, if shit hit the fan, she'd run.

Ohhh. A light bulb went off in her head. What if she

allowed herself to get caught? Then she could be taken to the place where Cy's sister was being kept. *Perfect!* Lila was proud of herself for coming up with that.

What if she was missing for a couple of days? She didn't want the Tiero to put together a search party for her. Maybe she should call Veila and let her know what she was doing.

No! Veila would start a fuss, try to help, attract attention, and definitely slow the process down.

She looked at her phone. Dead. *Doesn't matter.* Now she had the perfect excuse not to call Veila. Not calling Veila meant she didn't have to explain herself and couldn't be called back home.

She made herself comfortable, taking her heels off, pulling up a small box to sit on, ready for the long wait that might come.

Lila wasn't sure how long she waited. She catnapped as best as she could, with her nerves wound up. She heard voices. Not nearby, not yet, but the timbre told her the ones approaching were shifters. She crossed her fingers it wasn't Gavin and his bunch coming to retrieve her to take her home.

There were three voices, two male and one female.

CHAPTER TWELVE

"What's the plan?" Cy asked as he got into the SUV with Gavin and his men. He'd borrowed a shirt they had in the back. It was ill-fitting and tight, as the largest guy there was still smaller than Cy. He sat in the second row, next to another shifter.

Gavin, who sat shotgun, looked at Cy then at his men in the very backseat. He nodded. "We'll trace her."

"Got her," one of the guys in the back said, holding a phone up. "South side, next to the freeway, by Belton's."

"I know where that is." The driver jammed his foot on the gas pedal.

What the fuck? Cy was stunned, disbelieving. They were tracing her whereabouts? "Is that standard Tiero protocol? To trace the members of the family? To keep tabs on their whereabouts? Does she know?"

Gavin raised a brow, his expression saying it wasn't any of Cy's business. Then he began to speak anyway. "Since her sister was almost kidnapped a few weeks ago."

"Kidnapped?" That couldn't be a coincidence, could it? Petra missing and a Tiero shifter almost kidnapped? "Who did it?"

Gavin shook his head. "What's your name, shifter? Where are you coming from? What's your story?"

Cy looked out the window. *So much for anonymity. So much for not being a part of the shifter world.* After the shit he and Petra had gone through, all he wanted was to be left the fuck alone by all shifters. He didn't want to be friends with any—well, except one or two who had proven to be friends. It looked like saving his sister's—and now Lila's—lives would take a priority over his need for privacy.

"Cyric Villa." *Where from?* He didn't like discussing his life at all. He'd keep it brief. "North of here. I'm looking for my sister. That's all that matters about my story."

Gavin looked at the shifter in the seat next to Cy's.

Cy wondered if that look meant anything. "Now back to my question. Is it standard Tiero protocol to trace the members of the family?" Most importantly, he asked again, "Does she know?"

"No."

Cy contained the laughter threatening to spill out. Lila was going to pitch a fit when she found this out. He hadn't known her very long, but he had no doubt this wouldn't go over well. "Back to my question. Who tried to kidnap the Tiero sister?"

"Don't know yet. Sophie hasn't said much about it."

That wasn't much help at all. He wondered if Lila was having any better luck. Could her sister have told her anything about the kidnapping attempt? "Can you drive a little faster? Lives are at stake here."

"No, we don't want to attract the attention of the human authorities," Gavin responded.

Screw attracting attention. That was the last thing Cy worried about.

Twenty minutes later, the guy doing the tracking exclaimed, "Shit."

That was never a good thing.

"What's up?" Gavin asked him.

"I lost the signal. Completely."

"How does that work?" Cy turned to look at the guy.

"Dead battery or turning the phone off. It's not like we did anything that was too intrusive," Gavin answered for him.

Cy pondered the guy's response for a moment. "I think what that means is Lila's brother Vax may not know you're doing this."

"Security is my job. That means making occasional difficult calls on the spot."

"It also means Vax doesn't know, doesn't it?"

"He's busy."

"Yeah, and if he's pissed, your ass is in a sling."

"Look, shifter." Gavin managed to make it sound like an insult even though he was a shifter, too. "Your invitation could be rescinded at any point. It's not like we need you."

"I'd say maybe now that you can't track her, you may need me more than ever. I rate a 98 on the scenter scale." Cy knew, as shifter senses went, he could have been hiring his skills out for scenting. He would be willing to bet a lot of money Gavin didn't have anyone better as far as tracking went.

Gavin's nostrils flared just a bit, and a tic in his jaw reflected his irritation.

Cy was pretty sure he was right. "Got anyone better?"

"We sure don't," one of Gavin's men answered. "Best we have is a 78."

Gavin gave Cy a dirty look.

It was time to take control of the situation. "Enough said. Now I'll call a shot or two. Pull over and let me get out and scent. Don't stand near me. I don't need your scents interfering with Lila's." *Or my sister's, if I can find her scent here.*

The driver looked to Gavin for permission. Gavin nodded. The shifter pulled off the highway onto a side street.

"This is good. Stop here," Cy told him, then opened the car and got out.

Gavin opened his door, as did his group.

Cy looked at them. "Seriously. This much scent coming off all of you is going to hamper my abilities."

Gavin pointed to three men to get back in the vehicle, leaving only himself, Cy, and another shifter outside. Cy began to walk and raised his head, inhaling deeply.

Is that Lila? He turned to Gavin. "Give me more room."

"Hell, no," Gavin exclaimed.

He shrugged as though he didn't give a damn. "Fine. You can tell Vax Tiero how his sister wouldn't be dead if you weren't such a jealous ex-boyfriend."

"Fuck." A scowl crossed Gavin's features.

Nailed it. The fool should learn how to handle his emotions better when it came to Lila. Then again, Cy couldn't be sure he wouldn't be the same way about her. She was a hell of a woman.

Gavin stepped away, waving his man away, too. They both stood by the SUV while Cy kept walking. Without looking back to see if they were following, he rounded a corner and sprang into action.

45

Shifting into his tiger skin faster than he'd ever shifted before, and praying his block was still working, he jumped to a rooftop, cleared it in two leaps, and had gone five buildings and three alleys farther in less than ten seconds.

He was rid of Gavin and his men. Another thing he hadn't told them was he was extremely quick at running. He'd spent his life training to stay alive, so he wouldn't lose his life or let Petra's by being taken by shifters the way their parents' lives had been.

Yes, Cy was self-trained, but he pursued his with a single-minded focus that was rarely matched.

He didn't stop once he'd cleared that distance, only pausing long enough to raise his head, his tiger nostrils flaring, his lungs filling with air.

Lila!

He had her scent!

CHAPTER THIRTEEN

The voices came closer and closer. Their timbre definitely identified them as shifters. As far as she could tell, there were two males and one female. All shifters.

Their tones were friendly, so whatever was going on, it wasn't hostile. Maybe it was a dead end. Maybe it was just a few shifter friends, hanging out and walking down the street.

She rolled her eyes. Damn the luck. She tuned out their conversation, no longer interested.

Lila relaxed her pose, dropped her guard, and became comfortable again, waiting for the shifters to pass.

Except the shifters didn't pass. Their footsteps approached then stopped.

Lila refocused her attention. *Where'd they go?*

A click was followed by laughter. The door opened, letting a little street light in. From her vantage point, Lila could see three shifters, two large males, the third a female. The males were wolves. The female was a fox.

"Where's the party?" the fox shifter asked. Her tone was confused but not alarmed; clearly, she trusted the men.

"We're going to take you to it," one of the males said.

The way he said it made Lila's skin crawl. She didn't like this at all.

"What do you mean?" The fox shifter looked from one wolf shifter to the other. "I thought you said—"

"Don't worry about what he said." The other shifter's voice was gruff. He pulled something out of his pocket.

"Don't hurt her. We need her to be able to fight," the first wolf said.

"Fight?" The redhead's voice was shrill, panic kicking in.

Oh, shit. God. Now what? Lila had to help her. What was he was holding? A tranq, that was what it was. *Shit. Shit. Shit.*

They'd said fight. *Yes!* She'd found the right ones! She was happy. That meant she was in the right place. She wished Cy were here as backup. Hell, she'd even take Gavin's help. *Damn, damn, damn.*

Eager to help the fox shifter and not thinking about consequences, Lila stepped out from her hiding place before she could come up with a plan. In her mind, her tigress growled a warning at her lack of planning.

Her mind ran through some scenarios in the few seconds she was exposed but unnoticed by the wolf shifters.

She took pity on the fox. Lila could save her and then sacrifice herself in exchange. She'd be a decoy so the fox was freed. Then she'd let them take her, even though she'd be pretending to fight.

Great idea. Well, no, her tigress rumbled, not really, but it was the best she could come up with and these guys were going to overtake the fox shifter in a moment.

The fox struggled against the large wolf shifters, trying to pull her arms free.

"Don't make us hurt you, little fox." One of the wolves smiled a wicked grin.

"James." The other wolf pointed to Lila.

"What?" the one called James growled.

"We have company," the second shifter said.

All three shifters looked at Lila.

She glared at them. "Let her go."

"Oh, she's a fine, bossy one, isn't she, Will?" James asked the other shifter.

"Yes, but she's a tiger. We don't need another tiger."

"Don't be stupid," James said. "The other tiger won't last forever. She's fighting in three days. After that, they'll need another one." He leered at Lila.

"Run, fox," Lila told the female then shifted.

Now let's see how they like this.

CHAPTER FOURTEEN

Cy could tell Lila was close. Her scent grew stronger with each moment, with each step. He leaped over a fence and found himself in front of a Honda parked at a convenience store. It had to be hers; it carried her scent too strongly. He shifted into his human skin in case he was spotted.

If he thought he had problems now, wait until the humans sent out an alarm for a loose tiger. That was a problem he didn't need.

Looking into her car, he saw nothing that gave him any idea where she had gone or what she was doing. Well, hell, at least he knew she couldn't be far. She wouldn't have left her car behind.

Then it occurred to him. She wouldn't have left her car behind willingly.

Shit. What if she'd left it unwillingly? What if she'd been taken? Like Petra? He was more and more convinced this was exactly what had happened to Petra.

Could he follow Lila's scent to find Petra? Would that work?

He shifted back into his tiger skin and leaped over the eight-foot-tall fence, once more tracking her by scent. *Come on, Lila,* he begged her in his mind. *Where did you go? Where are you?*

Halting, he scented for her, to see if anything had changed. That was when he picked them up.

Shifters!

More of them.

The sound of a scuffle came from...

That way! He started off at a swift pace, reaching a warehouse. Inside. That's where it was, whatever it was.

The sounds of wood breaking, and things being thrown or run into were overwhelming.

He shifted into his human skin quickly and opened the door.

A figure bolted out of the warehouse, bowling him over.

Together, he and the figure—a fox?—rolled then came to a sudden stop, the fox on top of him. A female fox, who jumped up and took off at a run.

He sprang to his feet. That was one of the scents. Two more remained. Males. Wolves.

He shifted into his tiger and ran through the open door.

Bloody, fighting, teeth bared, claws swiping, Lila was taking on the two huge wolves. He couldn't sync with her; there was no time.

She was down on the ground, and one of the wolves was going for her throat.

Cy pounced on the wolf. Taking his throat in his jaws, he

pulled him off Lila. The other wolf attacked Lila, also going for her throat.

Christ, had she pissed them off or what? He let go of the first wolf, who made a dash for the door. Just as he reached for the second, mid-leap, the wolf changed course, abandoned his quest for Lila's throat and followed the first wolf through the door.

Lila shifted into her human skin. Her clothing was askew, her hair in disarray, and she bled from lacerations and bites all over her body.

Cy wasn't worried. She wouldn't die, and those wounds would heal, as shifters healed at an exponentially fast rate—if they hadn't been killed, that was. But she must have been in a lot of pain.

Then he saw her face. That was not the face of a woman in pain.

Now he was worried. He shifted into his human as well.

"What the hell are you doing?" Lila spun around completely, advancing on him as if he were an enemy.

"A thank you would be a more appropriate response," he growled.

"You-you-you fool!" She made fists and clenched them by her sides. Enraged, she flung herself at him, her fists flying, adrenaline clearly still racing throughout her body.

"You can't be serious. What the hell is wrong with you?" Cy grabbed her arms, holding her wrists. He pulled her hands down, kept them in front of her, at the same time pulling her close until their bodies almost touched. "Why didn't you fight them like you're fighting me?"

She yanked on her hands to pull them away, but his grip was like a vise. "I wanted them to catch me, goddammit. I wanted them to take me captive, so I can see if your sister is with them."

He paused, shaken. *What if I lose her?* The only woman he'd ever had a reaction to? The only woman he and his tiger had ever wanted? "I won't allow that."

"You can't stop me." Her voice was a vehement hiss. "I'm tired of males trying to tell me what the hell I can do."

This woman was divinely sexy. His tiger roared for her tigress. Their being so close together, their bodies almost touching, was too much for his tiger.

He lowered his head, his breathing rapid, his pulse pounding in his veins, his desire a primal beat that demanded to claim its mate.

With every breath he took, he sucked in her breath, merging his and hers as one, her essence deep in his lungs, flowing through his body.

She wet her lips, her pink tongue darting from one corner of her delicious mouth to the other. The sight made his cock strain and his tiger roar, and his hands gripped her tighter.

She winced. He released her a bit, not letting her go, being careful not to hurt her.

He looked into those emerald eyes with a fire behind them. Her lips parted slowly, as if in anticipation. Her breath stopped coming out, like she was holding it.

His chest clenched, and he lowered his head even more, pushing her backward with his body until he was pressing her into a crate, holding her prisoner against his torso.

He knew he should take it slow, but slow was the last thing he had in mind—unless it was slowly driving his cock into her while she flexed around his shaft.

Everything faded around him. The lust and need he had

for her put them in a spotlight, just him, just her. Nothing else mattered. Wrapping his other hand around her neck, he pulled her close until her nipples pressed against his body, insistent beads begging for attention.

His lips sealed hers, claiming her, branding her, needing her. His demanding tongue separated the seam of her lips, plundering her mouth the way he wanted to plunder every part of her body. The way he wanted to have his cock, his fingers, his tongue, every part of him, in every part of her.

CHAPTER FIFTEEN

Lila's body betrayed her. Hell, her body, her mind, and her tigress betrayed her. She let out a low moan when Cy's tongue entered her mouth, surrendering her tongue to his, becoming one with him in one of the most simple ways—and yet it made an impact on her as surely as if he'd had his brand of ownership tattooed on every part of her.

She'd never felt this before. Strong hands surrounded her, holding her, keeping her safe.

Her tongue met his in a tango of passion, dancing, sparring, making promises, assurances, and raising the temperature in her body. A flush took over, one that swarmed through her.

She pulled back, confused by the overwhelming surge of emotions. "Let me go. I—"

He cut off her words with a hard kiss, demanding more from her, taking nothing less than her complete surrender. Her head felt like a million bees filled it, buzzing around in a frenzy.

"I will never let you go."

Had any other man said that to Lila, she'd have shifted and gone for his throat. There was something about Cy. Knowing he could control her, the uncontrollable one, the one who never gave herself fully to a man—that was exactly what her tigress had been gravitating toward.

His tongue flicked at her lower lip. "Understood?" His hand tightened around hers. His other hand dropped to her lower back and pressed her against his hardness.

She sucked in a breath, her moisture building up and dropping quickly.

She could smell his desire, and she could see he could smell hers. His dark-brown tiger's eyes flared, glowing, ready to mate.

Still, the independent part of her wanted to balk. She narrowed her eyes at him. She touched the tip of her tongue to his lips and traced the outline of their perfectly sculpted fullness.

"I'm not some meek—"

He swooped down, and his tongue entered her mouth, sealing her words, leaving them unspoken. He forged in, dominating her tongue, tempting her with his sexiness.

He pulled back. "I know exactly what you are. Fierce, passionate, loyal. I want every part of you. I want to be in every part of you. Forever."

A jolt ran through her body. It started somewhere in her forehead and ran straight to her sex, traveled down to her toes, then back up to her breasts.

Goddammit. She had no control over that, and—*rawr*—she hated it! She jerked her hands free and shoved his chest, pushing him away. "What the hell are you doing?"

"I've just found you. I won't lose you. Unless you want me gone."

No. *No!* And yet she couldn't tell him that. Why was she so screwed up?

"Let's find your sister."

"Deny all you want. You won't belong to another."

CHAPTER SIXTEEN

Way to go. Cy cursed himself. He had no control when it came to her. A little bit of adrenaline from a fight and a little bit—okay, a lot—of desire for her, and he was gone. Off the deep end. If he didn't have to find Petra, he'd have bent her over that crate and taken her right then. He had no control with her.

Damn, her lips had tasted amazing and the scent rising from between her legs hadn't helped matters, throwing him even deeper into the abyss of desire.

"So, you say I screwed up your plan. What was it? Can we put it back together?"

"I overheard them. They say they have a tiger, and that she's fighting in three days. At first, they didn't want me. Then they did because they said, after three days, they wouldn't have a tiger." Her expression saddened. "I'm sorry. I can only think it's your sister they're talking about."

"On the bright side, they won't hurt her for three days. On the dark side of it, we only have three days to get her back.

They laughed because they said Dallas girls must be weak, since I didn't seem to be much of a fighter and Petra was easy to take."

"You? Not a fighter?"

She looked down, like she wasn't sure if she should be proud of herself or not. "I held back so they could catch me." She frowned at him. "Until you had to come in and screw up my plan by rescuing me."

"Sorry." He tried to look like he was sorry, but he wasn't sure if he should be or not. She could have been killed. "You really don't know for sure if they'd have taken you or killed you."

"I do. Maybe at first, they thought of killing me, but I think they look at things in terms of money, and I was money. Now we have to figure out a way to run into them again." She waggled a finger at him. "And you have to stay out of the way while I get caught."

"Like I said, I won't lose you. I can't. It's this thing. This connection I have with you. My tiger knew the first time he heard your heartbeat."

"My tigress knew, too. It took me a little longer." There was a twinkle in her eyes.

"Liar." He smiled, enjoying this side of her.

"I do want to get to know you better," she admitted, her voice low, as if she didn't believe she was saying it. "Let's save your sister then we'll see. Deal?"

He looked at her. Something about this woman pulled at him, and it was more than their tigers.

"Deal." As if he had a choice. He wasn't letting her go, not for any reason. Then Gavin flashed through his mind. He hoped for Gavin's sake their relationship was a part of the past.

59

Lila looked at him. Why did it feel like she'd known him all her life? Was this their tigers? Was their pull strong enough? She'd never felt anything like this before.

It was time to tell him her idea. Would he be like most men she'd known, or would he listen? "I think I have a plan."

He retrieved her shoes, picked her up around the waist, and set her on a tall crate. Taking one shoe, he wrapped his large hands around her foot and fitted the heel on her.

"I'm listening." He glanced up at her.

She couldn't look away from his lips, perfect and full. They offset his predator eyes, making her want to feel those lips on hers again.

He put the other shoe on her foot. Lila was so mesmerized by this act, the sensuousness with which he held her foot, the way he let his thumb glide over her arch, caressing her skin, it almost made her forget what she meant to say.

"What's the plan?" He helped her off the crate.

"I'll get us some block from my brother's place. He's got

enough for an army. Then I'll meet you in The Woodlands, down by the waterway and the pavilion."

"I don't like the idea of you going anywhere on your own."

"Yeah? Well, how did you get away from Gavin, and what's the likelihood he'll let you go if he sees you again?"

"Damn. You have a point." He told her about how he'd slipped away from Gavin and his men.

"I rest my case. They'll never let you go again. Plus, this way, if one of us gets caught, the other one will still be out and able to help, or at least rescue Petra."

"What if you get caught by those wolves, and this time you piss them off? I don't like this plan at all."

"Look, Cy." She took his hand. "Gavin's not going to help you, and he's not going to help me help you."

"Because you dumped him?"

"Yes—Wait, how did you know?" Had Gavin told Cy something? She fumed Gavin might have misled him.

"Call it a hunch."

She eyed him suspiciously. "That's a pretty lucky hunch."

He shrugged.

She continued, "I can't call my brother. I don't want to." But... why didn't she want to call Vax? She couldn't think of a good reason. Maybe she just wanted to be someone other than a girl who had to be saved. Not that Vax would treat her that way, or ever had, but her father had always made her feel like girls were second best to boys. *Wow. Maybe I'm pretty fucked up.*

Nah, her father was the one who was pretty fucked up. "Just get to Houston alive. I'll meet you in The Woodlands, by the waterway, around by the pavilion. Think you can find it?"

"I'll find your scent." He kissed her lips, his tongue tempting her with promises.

CHAPTER EIGHTEEN

Cy walked Lila to her car, and she got in and started it. As she watched him in the rearview mirror, a wave of sadness washed over her. There was something about leaving him behind that bothered her and her tigress.

Be careful, she mouthed, knowing he couldn't hear her.

She made it back to Tiero Tower One in less than thirty minutes. After pulling into her spot in the parking garage, she slipped her key into the elevator to unlock it. She had to use a different key to go to her own floor. Pressing the button, she tapped her heel on the tile, impatient and very, very ready to get on the road again.

She exited the elevator and almost ran into one of Gavin's men standing by the door.

"Hi, Grayson." She waved nonchalantly, as though she hadn't been through a bunch of shit tonight, and as though her dress wasn't torn and bloody.

"Lila." He nodded his acknowledgment then immediately turned and started to talk into an earpiece.

She didn't think she'd be lucky enough for him to be taking to a girlfriend. Oh, hell, no. She was willing to put money on it he was reporting in to Gavin. Damn the luck. Still, without acting too suspicious, she walked nonchalantly to her apartment.

There was no time for a shower, so she wet a washcloth and ran it over the bloody areas, sponging off the scars that had formed.

Done, she slipped into a pair of jeans, stopping to check out her ass in the mirror, wiggling to get a better fit. Next, a black T-shirt, some black boots, and she was good to go.

Shit! She'd forgotten the block. She'd run up to Vax's office —she knew where he kept his stash. Once she'd grabbed her keys, her cell—and her charger, for goodness's sake—she opened the door and ran out.

Damn!

She ran into a broad chest in a crisp white shirt and a jacket.

She bounced back.

Gavin.

Damn the luck.

CHAPTER NINETEEN

Cy shifted into his tiger skin and loped toward his vehicle. He'd left it on the outskirts of Dallas, on the north side, when he'd first arrived to Tiero territory. Quite a haul away. He had no choice; he was going to have to lope the whole way there. Time was of the essence.

He was torn. On one hand, he had to get to his sister immediately. Her three-day death sentence wasn't sitting well with him. On the other hand, the woman he would claim as his mate was going off on her own, into the same danger his sister was in. He didn't know she wasn't going to do something stupid that would get her killed.

His tiger growled.

Okay, he hadn't meant to think the word stupid. Maybe foolhardy was a better word. Or bold. Or crazy.

The tiger growled again. *Well, I'm not any happier than you are about her decision.*

"I'm thinking, I'm thinking." He pulled the SUV out of the parking lot he'd left it in. He hadn't even had time to catch his breath. "I think I have a solution." Why the hell was he talking to his tiger out loud? "Jeez, I've lost it."

His tiger rumbled in agreement.

He took his cell out and flipped through the contacts with his index finger. He'd call the only person he trusted.

His tiger rumbled in agreement again.

The phone's ring was shrill in his ear. "Come on, answer. Answer already." Finally, a connection was made.

"Hello?" The most welcoming voice he'd heard in a long time answered. It was the voice of someone who had become like a big sister or an aunt to him and Petra.

"Mae?"

"Cy?" He knew she was smiling from the way her voice changed. "How are you? How is Petra?" Then her voice turned serious. "I don't think it's a good thing that you're calling me, is it? What's going on?"

He could never hide anything from Mae Forester; she was practically psychic. He ran through the story of Petra's disappearance.

Mae spoke up. "Okay. Let me see how I can help."

"Wait. Mae. There's more."

She paused, and he could hear her breathing on the other end.

"There's a girl. Lila Tiero—"

"Vax's baby sister. Well, half-sister, to be precise."

"Yes! Well, she's trying to help, but I'm worried about her." He brought Mae up to speed with everything but how he felt about Lila.

"You don't have to tell me the rest," Mae said. "I can hear it in your voice. Let me make some calls."

"She's going to hate me for this. I don't think she likes being babied."

"I'll be sensitive to that when I make arrangements."

He blew out a breath and kept his foot steady on the gas. He fought back the urge to tell her how worried he was.

"Look, Cy, have I ever let you down?"

She was right, she hadn't. "Okay. Just keep me posted? Please? Lila means a lot to me."

Mae's tone softened. "I know, Cy. I know how hard it is for you to feel this, and I know how much harder it is for you to say it. We'll make sure your mate comes out of this unscathed."

"Wait, no, I didn't say she's my—"

The line went dead. Mae, as always, had hit the nail on the head. Even though she lived a ways from him in Bear Canyon Valley, she'd always been there for him and Petra. He owed her so much. If Mae called and asked him to help with anything, anything at all, he'd be on the road immediately.

He wondered how many shifters owed her.

Two hours plus, and more than a hundred miles later, Cy hadn't heard a word from Mae. He was more than halfway to Houston and had no clue what was going on. Worse, he didn't even have Lila's cell number. What the hell was wrong with him? Was his brain gone?

The not knowing was killing him. He called Mae, who answered on the first ring.

"I was just going to call you," she said.

"Catch me up. What have you done?" And how much would Lila hate him when this was all over?

"I called Vax."

Shit. That didn't bode well. The last thing Lila would want was her big brother rescuing her. "What did he say?"

"He called Gavin."

Ah, double shit. "And?"

"Vax told Gavin to give Lila whatever she wants to help her."

Maybe that wasn't so bad, after all. "Why do I have the feeling there's more?"

He kept his eyes on the road. A green sign in the grass by the roadside advised that Huntsville was a few miles away. Another sign warned him not to pick up hitchhikers as this was a prison area.

Lila would be driving through this? As long as her adversaries were human, she'd be fine. Throw a bunch of shifters into the mix, and Cy would be worried.

"The thing is," Mae explained, "the wolves in Houston, those are two brothers. Reese and Rory Nielsen. They have a whole slew of cousins. The cousins are a mangy bunch of outlaws from the Rafferty side of the Nielsen brothers. Something like their father's first cousin's offspring, or something like that. Who really knows? Bunch of mongrels, that's what they are."

Cy was confused. Where was all this going?

Mae continued, "So, Vax is not exactly available. He's out somewhere in the Gulf of Mexico, on one of his cousin Lézare's boats, vacationing with his new mate. So for him, getting back won't be quick."

"And..." he prodded her. Good grief, this wasn't like Mae, taking so long to get to the point.

"He made some calls. They really don't have a relationship with the Nielsen tribe, but Vax wanted to arrange for them to meet with you. He said Lézare would call and make nice, set the scene, or something to that effect." Mae paused, probably to breathe.

Of all the damned positions to be in! Cy had spent his adult life avoiding shifters, having nothing to do with them because he wanted to be left alone. He had no trust and no love for them. The last thing he wanted to do was put his or Petra's fate in the hands of shifters.

"Mae—"

"You have to do this. I know it's out of your comfort zone."

It was way more than out of his comfort zone. "What good will it do?"

"Lézare doesn't think the Nielsen brothers know what their cousins are doing. They'd be powerful allies in shutting down an illegal operation and getting Petra back."

"If they don't know what their cousins are doing," Cy added. "If."

"Lézare's a lot of things, but one thing he's got going for him, he's a powerhouse of information."

He shook his head. He would have to gamble his sister's life on that. A cool breeze washed over him, except there was no breeze. Perspiration broke out on his forehead.

"We'll see." He ended the call with Mae.

Maybe he should pursue some other options. At least he could forge on knowing Gavin would take care of Lila.

Gavin. His stomach roiled.

Her ex.

Gavin, who was still in love with Lila.

Cy clenched his jaw.

CHAPTER TWENTY

"Leave me alone." Lila glared at Gavin. "I've had enough of your interference." She tried to walk around him, but he shifted his weight, still blocking her. "Move."

"Wait." Gavin didn't move.

She was livid and tired of his always watching her, always *making sure you're okay.*

"What do you want?" She didn't even have enough patience to be polite.

"Vax called."

She rolled her eyes. Now Vax was going to start in on this bullshit? She was tired of being sheltered. First, her father when she was living in Europe, now Vax, here in America. It had gone on long enough. "And?"

He drew a deep breath, as if what he had to say was difficult. "He wants me to help you." Gavin swallowed, his Adam's apple bobbing. "I'm supposed to act as if anything you say is the same as coming from him."

69

Suspicious, she crossed her arms over her chest. "What else?"

"He and Callie won't make it back immediately. He said the next few days were crucial and I'm to be an asset, not an obstacle."

It felt like someone had released a thousand doves in Lila's chest. Her brother was trusting her. "So you have to do anything I say?"

"Anything except leave you unguarded." A smile crept to Gavin's face. "He knows your propensities."

Lila nodded.

"Lila." His expression softened. "I didn't mean to be such a—"

"Douche?" She finished his sentence.

"I was going to say I didn't mean to be so overly concerned about you."

"Douche works better." She smiled at him, cautious. Just because he'd apologized, that didn't mean he was going to change his ways or fall out of love with her. For all she knew, he said this to get her to let her guard down. "I'm going to get some block. I'm driving to Houston. Alone."

"We'll be behind you in the SUV."

"Lose the tracker."

"But—"

"Lose it."

He growled, deep in his chest. She ignored it. She'd gotten what she wanted so far.

"Meet you in the garage in ten."

CHAPTER TWENTY-ONE

There it was—a sign letting Cy know he was in The Woodlands, a few miles north of Houston. Now he had a choice to make. Had the choice already been made for him? He exited the freeway. He was going to meet Lila.

His tiger growled, ready for an argument.

Haven't you done enough interfering? This whole mate thing, the damned timing on it sucks. Cy couldn't control his temper.

If he met Lila, she'd be in danger, and he wouldn't be able to help her and Petra at the same time. Mae's plan was better. Letting Gavin secure Lila's safety while Cy looked for his sister was the more sound idea, even if he hated to admit it. Lila would hate him. They were supposed to do this together.

Damn it. He didn't have her number, so he could call her. *Jeez, would I even want to call her?* She'd do nothing but rant about how he was no different than the other males in her life. Rock and a hard place.

He had to meet the Nielsen brothers, and he had no assurances they hadn't been a part of the abduction. No one really knew them, except for Vax's cousin, and only by word of mouth. Cy couldn't put much faith into a pair of strangers. Bringing Lila here would be like putting her in the lion's den. Who would look after her when he had to go after Petra?

Fuck!

He pulled back onto the freeway, torn between the two options, though he knew meeting Lila wasn't really an option but more like bringing danger straight to her. He had to go forward with Mae's plan and meet the Nielsen brothers, but he'd rather Lila was not in danger while he was meeting with them.

Only one thing left to do. He called Mae.

"Sorry I'm a bother. I want to make sure there's no word on Petra and that Lila's okay. I'm in Houston, bound for the Nielsen place."

"She's fine. Gavin is keeping in touch with Vax and Lézare. They're keeping me posted. Though I have to tell you," Mae giggled, "it seems Gavin is still carrying a torch for Lila."

Cy's tiger growled. "I know." He wanted to tell Mae it was one-sided, but, after this betrayal he was serving up to Lila, she might not ever want to see him again.

Mae had said to drive to Sugarland then head out on 59. That part wasn't a problem for Cy; he was already on 59. She'd said he should get out of his vehicle any time after that, and if he could still scent as well as he had years ago, he'd have no problem finding the Nielsen tribe.

He refrained from bragging about his scenting and how it had gotten even better. Stepping out of the Rover as soon as he'd crossed through the busy, urbanized area of Sugarland, he took a deep breath.

The scent of shifters hit him hard. Many of them. They weren't hiding their presence, and they weren't using block. These shifters were staking out their territory and making sure any trespassing shifters knew it was Nielsen territory.

Mae's directions were to scent for them then head east.

East? Okay, so he'd find the first road he could turn on then turn east.

"Ride with your windows down," she said.

He'd laughed. "Now give me the real directions."

"Really, that will get *you* there, but here's the directions I'd give to someone who can't scent like you do. Turn left at the co-op, then right at a little private airport, then the second left. Follow the dirt road."

He did. Twenty miles later, he pulled onto the dirt road. Two miles after that, he stopped in front of a house that looked like a ranch house with a bunkhouse nearby, except the bunkhouse was as extravagant as the house. Both were mansions. A large barn at the very back of the property almost made it look like a working ranch. *Is it a working ranch*?

An intricately carved, reinforced metal gate blocked his entrance to the drive. He pulled up to the speaker in a red brick column. Before he could open his mouth, the gate began a slow, motorized hum and swung open.

Surely, they weren't expecting him? He never knew what to think when it came to Mae's involvement. She seemed to have connections all over the shifter world.

He inched the Rover in, keeping his guard up, the scent of wolves heavy in the air.

He parked on the covered driveway and turned the engine off, certain he was under electronic surveillance as well as the careful scrutiny of a security team.

He waited to see if he'd be greeted.

Nothing.

Cy opened his car door. He'd go into the dragon's lair himself, then, so to speak. More like the wolves' den.

CHAPTER TWENTY-TWO

L ila checked the charge on her phone. The battery was full. This time she wasn't going to let her phone run out of juice. She was at the exit for the pavilion, not far from the waterway. Her body buzzed with excitement. Was it because she was going to see Cy again?

Taking a right, she pulled into a parking lot near the pavilion, got out, locked her car, and made her way down to the waterway. She found a bench to sit on to wait. She didn't see Gavin, didn't know if he'd pulled in, didn't know if he was tracking her—he better not be. She inhaled, but picked up no sign of Cy, none at all. How could she have beaten him here?

Two hours later, she was still waiting. No Cy. This wasn't good. He'd had a head start. There was no reason he wouldn't have beaten her here, except...

She didn't want to think of the possibilities.

Now he was more than two hours late. A feeling churned in her gut. With every passing moment, the churning became more of a burn. Something had to be wrong. She needed to take action. But what kind of action?

Jesus. She had no plan B. No backup at all.

Her phone rang.

Cy! Could it be him? Before picking it up, she realized she had never given him her number. She looked at the screen.

Gavin.

Great timing. Just great. She pressed reject. She rejected his next call, too. On the third call, she figured out he wasn't going to stop until she answered.

"What?" She was snappy, with no interest in being sweet. "Don't come near me. Stay away. I'm going into Houston."

"If Cyric wanted you to find him, he wouldn't have called and had Vax tell me to watch over you while he went on to look for his sister."

"You're lying." It felt like someone had injected her veins with ice water. As soon as she told Gavin he was lying, she knew he wasn't. Why else would Cy not be here? How else would Gavin know to even say that? A cold fury burned through her. How dare Cy do this to her? How dare he minimize her?

She stormed off toward her car and got in. Headlights went on across the street in a parallel parking lot. A large, oversized SUV. Gavin. She resisted the urge to flip him off.

She'd find Cy herself. She'd save his sister, and she'd kick his ass. Then she'd go home and get in the hot tub and drink a bottle of wine. Alone.

Men. She huffed.

Bastards.

Lila knew Gavin was following her. She also knew that

once she got into the downtown area, she could ditch him easily. So she went alone, making sure they could keep up, allowing them a false sense of security.

She picked a random downtown exit that looked as good as any then exited, headed down the street, took a few lefts and rights, and finally pulled into a parking garage. As soon as she was in, she cut the wheel to the right sharply and pulled into a spot that looked more like a cubbyhole. It wasn't even a full parking place. She killed her lights, shut off her car and waited, holding her breath and controlling her pulse.

Seconds later, the dark SUV crept by, heading into the bowels of the parking garage, secure in the knowledge she'd gone that way.

She smirked, jumped out, and headed to a stairwell. Taking the stairs, she went to the second floor and shifted. Her sleek tiger form bounded across the parking garage, leaped out of the opening between concrete slabs, and landed on the ground below. In a few more bounds, she was across the dark and isolated alley and shifting back.

She wandered around downtown, pausing to check for shifter scents. How could there be none? How could she be in the middle of downtown Houston and not pick up a single shifter? Her feet hurt, and her patience was wearing thin.

An hour later, just as she was about to pick up her cell phone and look for other options, she caught the scent of a shifter.

No! Two! *Eureka*. Surely that would lead her somewhere, if only to a place where she could ask questions.

She let her senses lead her as she followed the scents. *Wolves. Male.* She couldn't get that lucky, could she?

She took a corner and—

She was that lucky.

Or unlucky, depending.

Will and James. Her face surely showed the distaste she felt toward the two shifters.

"Look who's trespassing," one of them said. She wasn't sure which. Stringy hair in dire need of a shampoo and a cut, lanky builds, and bad teeth characterized their appearance and made them identical.

"Go away, creeps." She sneered at them. "Or do you want more of what you got last time?"

"Where's your big boyfriend today?" One of them looked behind her while the other put his hand on her arm.

She shrugged him off. "Not my boyfriend."

"No? Want one?" He ran his thick tongue over swollen, chapped lips.

Lila's stomach protested, pitching and tossing bile into her mouth.

"Maybe she likes me better," the other one said, winking at her.

"Maybe you should both fuck off."

Chapped Lips raised his hand and backhanded her before she could react. She stumbled backward. The other one grabbed her while Chapped Lips put his hand behind his back.

When he pulled it out, he held a tranq. Kicking at his hand, Lila missed, tripped, and tried to right herself.

A sting in her thigh heralded the bad news. He'd pierced her skin with the tranq's needle.

"You son of a bitch." She stumbled forward.

"Catch her, asshole. She's useless if she's lame or wounded."

Arms wrapped around her as she pitched forward. The gray concrete was an out-of-focus blur.

CHAPTER TWENTY-THREE

Cy looked around the carport, studying the back door. Should he go around to the front? Or was it better to knock here? He closed his car door quietly.

Before he could make a decision a number of wolf shifters exited through the back door. He counted seven. Then two more brought up the rear. These were larger, blond shifters, also wolves.

The two blond shifters were identical twins, in fact. They looked him up and down, their expressions stoic, and their scent held no fear or no animosity. They looked at each other, then nodded.

"Cyric Villa?"

They knew his name? How the hell did that work? Mae must have told them, but would that make them friendly or enemies? He nodded. "And you?"

One of the wolf shifters pointed to the other one. "He's Rory." He pointed to his own chest. "I'm Reese Nielsen. You're in our territory."

Oh shit. The whole trespassing thing was going to get ugly now. "Yeah, about that. I'm—"

"Both Lézare and Mae called. We know," Rory said. "Thing is, it doesn't sound right. Who are these shifters who attacked your girl?"

"Skinny. Ratty looking. Lanky, stringy hair."

Reese grimaced. "You just described half of the Rafferty cousins. We'd disown them if we had one good reason. They're our father's cousins, distant."

Rory shook his head. His short blond hair was spiked; his eyes were a piercing blue.

"I need to find them. I'm not here to insult your family, but they have my sister."

"You? One shifter? Alone?" Reese made a tsk-ing sound. "That's not good odds. There's probably ten of them out there."

Cy narrowed his eyes. Now he was getting somewhere. "Out where?"

"Oh, they're squatting on some land east of our territory. Between Lake Charles and Beaumont." Rory looked at Reese. "I don't think they have the facilities to house something like what you told Mae you heard."

"I'm pretty sure we'd have heard if they were building something like that," Reese agreed.

"I'll give them a call." Rory took out a cell phone and tapped the screen. Several taps later, he put the phone back in his pocket. "No answer."

"They know better," Reese said.

"I need to find my sister." Cy's phone vibrated in his pocket. He was tempted to ignore it, but it could be important. He looked at the screen.

81

Mae.

"Excuse me," he said to the wolf shifters and gestured to his phone, turning slightly from the shifter twins. "Hey," he said into the phone.

"Lila's missing." Mae's voice was laced with concern.

"What do you mean, missing? Gavin's got his eyes on her, right?"

"He lost her."

Cy's world crumbled. Now Lila was gone, too. "Got to go, Mae. I'll call you later." He turned to the brothers. "Now Lila Tiero is missing, too. Do you still want to talk about this, or can I go find them?" He felt grim. "Can I get directions now?"

"I don't think that's wise," Rory said.

Cy bit back a sigh of exasperation, controlled his pulse, and fought his temper. "I don't have time to debate this. Last night they said the fight would be in three days. By my estimation, now it's two. That means it's the day after tomorrow. I don't know what time, and I can't take a chance." He unclenched his jaw. "Do you have anything more specific for me?"

"Look at this one," Rory said to Reese, pointing to Cy. "He's brave, but we can't let him go out there. Those jackal Raffertys will kill him."

"Too many of them, too little of him."

Cy turned his back on them, done with conversation, uncaring if he was rude. He reached for the Rover's door handle.

"We'll drive," one of them said. It sounded like Rory.

Cy turned back toward them.

"We owe Lézare," Reese said. "So let's take care of him. Lézare said Mae Forester would be appreciative."

"She's a good one to have on your side," Rory added.

What the hell. Was there any shifter who didn't think so? Cy didn't bother with small talk. "I'm ready to go."

"Pull your Rover into the barn. We're taking ours."

CHAPTER TWENTY-FOUR

The first thing Lila noticed was her head felt like someone had emptied her brain out and filled her skull with cotton candy. She couldn't concentrate; it was as if she was flying in clouds. At first, she thought she was dreaming. The last thing she remembered was those assholes Will and James, and they'd been holding a tranq. How long had she been out? Was she alone?

She opened her eyes. The room was dark. Thank God for tiger vision. She was in a cage, not unlike the cage Cy had been held in, except this one was smaller, and the bottom half was solid metal. Moving slowly, unsure who could see her and not wanting to alarm anyone, she stretched her legs. At least the cage was long enough for her to stretch out.

She turned her head slowly, looking around. There were several cages in the large room, all with the same solid metal sheath surrounding the bottom half.

The room was tall and large, close to the size of a basketball court. Bleachers lined the walls.

The smell of blood, old and new, filled her lungs. Her stomach pitched in protest to the vileness. The scent of shifters was pervasive, merging with the smell of blood. There'd been others in here. Maybe they still were. *Concentrate*, she told herself, *and think calmly*. That wasn't easy when part of her wanted to panic and scream in horror. She'd pay attention to her tiger senses.

Lila felt out of her element. Relying on her tiger senses for security had not been the way she'd grown up. She'd always had her father's security team around. Then when she'd moved to America with Vax, she'd had his team to take care of her. Now she had to do it on her own. Her tigress emitted a low growl of assurance. Lila wished she felt as secure.

She was used to dealing with drunks in After Dark and city thugs. This ordeal of killing shifters for sport and using her tiger senses to survive was new to her.

Time to tiger up and take care of herself.

And Petra!

Jeez, she'd almost forgotten in her panic she was here to save Petra.

She listened for heartbeats and found several. Some beat weakly, and a couple were strong. Where were these others? Were they captives like her? In cages? Or were they guards to keep her from escaping?

How would she escape from a metal cage, anyway? She had way too many questions and needed answers. First things first—were the other cages empty?

Lila rose to her knees to get a better view into the other cages, but couldn't see over the solid metal sheets covering the lower halves. She tiptoed near the back of her cage, stood at her full height, and tried to glimpse into the other cages.

She still couldn't see. She coughed low, hoping whoever heard her wasn't an enemy.

"Hello?" a soft female voice said. "Are you awake? You were unconscious when they brought you in."

Was that foe or friend? "Who are you?" Lila looked to her left, where the voice had come from.

"Petra Villa."

Lila's heart almost jumped out of her chest with excitement. She fought to hold in the squeal wanting to come out. Keeping her voice low, she said, "Cy is looking for you. I'm helping him."

"Cy doesn't like shifters." Petra's voice was suspicious. "He doesn't work with them."

"I guess you can tell him that yourself, since he's working with me." *Or is he?* Lila wondered, since he was not only working with Gavin, he'd stood her up at the pavilion.

"So where is he, then?" Petra still sounded suspicious, but not as much.

"He's..." Now what was Lila going to say? "We got separated." That wasn't a lie. They had gotten separated, and it would seem they were separated in more than one way.

"I hope he gets here before tonight. I'm scheduled to fight."

A shiver passed over Lila, one that came with panic. "Tonight? I thought it was tomorrow night?"

"It was moved up."

"Where are we?"

"Some underground facility. That's all I know. Every few days they have fights." Petra sniffled. "The shifters are killed. Totally. Dead."

"Wait. How can that be? We can't be—"

"Their heads are cut off. Their shifter animal dies with them."

Shit. That *was* the way to kill a shifter. "Humans do this?"

"No. It's run by shifters, but the spectators are humans and shifters."

"And these humans know about us?" Lila couldn't wrap her head around it.

Soft sobs came from Petra. "I made a friend. He's gone. He was a lion shifter. He... I don't think he had a tribe. Three days ago he was taken to fight."

Rustling noises and some shuffling came from Petra's direction. Then she stood. Dark hair framed Petra's dark, tear-filled eyes.

Lila studied the other woman. Her face was drawn, and her eyes had dark circle half-moons beneath them.

Petra shivered and wrapped her arms around herself. "I know he's dead."

"I'm sorry." Lila put her hand through the bars, reaching for Petra's, hoping they could span the distance. Petra's cold fingertip touched hers. "Let's get out of here."

"There's no way. Today is the day I die." She looked down.

"You can't die today. You're too young." That came from another voice. A woman raised her head.

Lila studied the leopard shifter. "How long have you been here?"

"Four weeks. They're waiting for me to heal so I can go into the arena." The leopard shifter raised an arm wrapped in bandages. "I wouldn't make much of an opponent with my injury. The patrons wouldn't get their money's worth." She smiled something that looked more like a grimace. "I'm Maia."

A loud crash came from the distance. It sounded like it was on the other side of the door.

"They're coming," Petra said. "Get down. They don't like it when we talk." She and the leopard vanished.

Lila dropped down in her cage and huddled, her legs tucked close to her body, her chin on her knees. A heavy-sounding door creaked open. Lila heard loud footsteps, and, a moment later, Will and James were in front of her cage.

She didn't even pretend to be asleep.

"Our newest guest is awake," one of them said. She still didn't know which one was which.

"Where am I?" she demanded.

"Don't worry about it. It doesn't matter, does it, James?" His laughter sounded more like a cackle. Clearly, this one was Will.

"Why doesn't it matter? Let me go. I can get you some money. A lot of it."

"I doubt that." James licked his chapped lips, his saliva making them shiny and purplish.

Lila couldn't handle looking at his face. She glanced down, studying his boots. "I'm a Tiero. My brother would pay a lot to see me freed, and her, too."

"Ooooh, a Tiero," Will mocked her. "Too bad the little orange tiger is spoken for. We promised a tiger tonight, and we're delivering one."

"Anyway," James added, "we make good money doing this. Way more than your brother can pay. Who wants to deal with a bunch of pissed-off Tieros when they find out we have you? Nah, you're better off here, where no one will know who you are. You'll just be another contestant in our games."

"Then let me fight in her place. She's not a fighter." Lila pointed to Petra's cage.

"No, we've already printed up the schedules. A tiger fighting a bear. That's final." James crossed his arms, his face resolute.

"What's it to you, anyway?" Will said.

"I'm a tiger. What's the problem? I'm a white tiger. That should create a buzz for you. Wouldn't your guests rather see a white tiger?"

"Shut up." Will's voice was whiny. "You don't tell us how to run our business."

James put his hand on Will's arm. "Wait. Let me see. What do you think, Will? Could we get a higher premium?"

Will scratched his head, the greasy hair moving in entire sections. "Do it. Call the boss."

Lila wanted to cheer. She stepped closer to the cage's door. Now they were getting somewhere, and maybe she could get some information. "Who's your boss?"

"Nunya. You know what that means?" Will said while James walked away, tapping on a cell phone.

James returned a moment later, a smile on his face. "I think we might make the boss happy." He took a set of keys out of his pocket. "Let's go, white tigress. The boss wants to see you. We're taking you there." He looked at Will. "Leave the orange tiger here. Bring the white."

Lila moved farther back in the cage, away from the two wolf shifters. "No. Bring the orange, too. I won't go without her."

"You don't call the shots, you bossy bitch."

Petra screamed and lunged for the wolf. He pulled something out of his pocket and reached for Petra. Lila lunged forward, her hands between the bars, and just managed to knock the tranq out of his hands, but not before he'd stuck Petra briefly. Had he gotten the tranq into her?

"Who the hell do you think you are?" Will snapped at Lila.

Bright lights went on overhead.

"What the hell?" James turned around, looking for the intruder.

A crowd of shifters walked in behind two identical blond, powerfully built wolf shifters. Amongst them were Gavin and his men, an assortment of other species, and Cy.

Cy, who sauntered in alone, stood tall and quiet, and looked like a volcano of emotions.

"I'll tell you who she is. She's my sister," Lila's brother Vax announced, coming forward, between all the shifters.

They parted to let him come to the front. He stood in front of Lila's cage.

"And my cousin," a man said. Tall, dark, handsome. Lila was confused. Who was this man? "Lézare Arceneaux." He winked and sent her a devilish grin.

He was the one Vax had told her about. The one who had helped with Natalya.

"And my—" Cy stepped forward from behind Lézare and Vax. He didn't finish his sentence.

A fury built in Lila, fueled by how much she'd already fallen for the tall, striking, powerful Siberian tiger shifter.

Vax gave Cy a double take, as if he was wondering what he was going to say.

Lila glared at Cy. She knew what he'd almost admitted.

CHAPTER TWENTY-FIVE

Cy was going to say the word *mate*, until he saw the daggers Lila was flinging at him with her dark, sexy eyes. A fury burned behind her expression. He had screwed up when he hadn't let her in on this, and look where it had gotten them. She was in a worse position, prisoner of these two asshole wolf shifters. She could have ended up dead.

He glanced at his baby sister. She was pale and it seemed she'd lost weight. Dark circles emphasized the ordeal she'd been through. "Petra."

Petra sat slumped in the corner of her cage. "Cy." Her voice was a weak whisper. "Those wolves were going to make me fight a bear." Her words grew slower and slower. "They kill shifters."

He turned to eye at the two wolf shifters he'd encountered in Dallas. They were the same ones who fought with Lila. The ones he'd driven off. Fury blazed a trail throughout his body. Rage made him and his tiger want to take their lives.

The two stringy-looking wolf shifters began to sputter in an attempt to speak.

"Shut up, you damned hillbilly jackals," Rory said.

CHAPTER TWENTY-SIX

L ila was still locked in this damned cage, and poor Petra
 sat slumped, almost unconscious. She should have
been out by now, but maybe they'd emptied the tranq into her.

"Shut up, you damned hillbilly jackals," said a tall, blond
wolf shifter.

"You're not worthy of being called wolves," came from
another wolf shifter, identical to the first.

One of the blond wolf shifters indicated Petra's cage with
a nod.

Will opened the door. Cy wrapped his arms around Petra,
cradling her.

"Let me out. Now." Lila was sick and tired of being in this
cage, and in this filthy, smelly building. "I'm going home."

As soon as she came out of the cage, she stuck her finger in
Cy's chest. "You had Gavin assigned to babysit me?" She shook
her head. "Unbelievable."

She strolled past Vax. She wasn't even going to tell him

how what he'd done hurt her. He didn't trust her to take care of herself.

Vax had a weird smile plastered on his face. Irritation poked at her the way someone would poke at a wild beast with a stick. She almost gave her brother a piece of her mind; instead, she kept walking straight ahead, not looking at anyone. She had no plan and didn't care if she had to crawl home. She was furious and beyond reasoning.

Lila stomped past the shifters, cages, and bleachers, stopping in front of a large door. She yanked on the handle and stormed out of the building. Outside, the late afternoon sun painted everything in shades of golden orange. A grove of trees a few yards away flanked a dirt road.

She had no idea where she was or where she was going. She paused to get her bearings, her pulse and adrenaline still racing from the driving fury. She'd just stroll on the side of the road until she could get a ride to... whatever was closer, her car or home.

She didn't realize she'd been followed until a strong pair of arms swooped her into a firm hold.

She opened her mouth to yell, but before she could, she was swung over a wide shoulder, landing with a hard *oomph*, ass up. The breath was knocked from her body, rendering her unable to fight or even move for a moment.

It didn't take her long to figure out who the wide shoulders belonged to, especially not when she could see the ass attached to the body, within arm's reach. Only one man would dare to do this to her.

"Put me down. Now." She clenched her hands into fists, ready to pummel on a muscle-bound back.

Instead of putting her down, he strolled toward the trees she'd seen when she'd first gone outside. Cy didn't say a word.

She squirmed to get out of his grip, but it merely tightened around her thighs, binding her closer to him. She hit him, blow after blow, and he kept on going, impervious to any pain she might have caused. She stopped hitting him and grabbed onto his waistband, trying to use it as leverage to pull herself out of his grip. And again, his hold on her grew tighter.

A few paces later, they reached the grove. He entered between the trees, his footing sure on the uneven ground.

Winded from the exertion of squirming, and ready to save her energy for a last-ditch attempt at an escape, Lila stopped fighting and went still.

He pulled her off his shoulders with a self-assured and quick grip. Lila landed on her feet and would have stumbled if not for the hold he had on her arms.

"I hate you," she hissed.

"I know." He pushed her backward against a tree's rough bark and lowered his head.

"You didn't have any faith in me at all." The buildup of emotions rose in her chest. *No. Goddammit. No.* She wasn't going to cry. She wasn't going to be hurt that he didn't treat her like something more than a porcelain princess meant to be kept on a shelf. Her tiger rumbled in Lila's chest. *Shut up. Don't you dare take his side!* she screamed at her tigress in her mind.

Behind his obsidian eyes, an amber glow burned. His tiger. She didn't want to look at it, so she cast her eyes away toward a tree.

He lowered his head even more. "It's not you that I don't have faith in." His words were a low, tortured whisper.

His lips touched hers, their softness a contradiction to the hardness of his body as he pressed against her, pushing her into the tree. He pulled back, his eyes on her face, studying, memorizing.

Lila's body betrayed her, obeying her tigress instead, as her breasts swelled to press closer to his body. Her nipples peaked into a hardness that buzzed throughout her body. The current coursing in her limbs, pulse, and sex was synchronized and reverberating. It was as if she held the world's largest seashell to her ears, because it felt like she could hear the ocean's rush.

His cheek pressed against hers. She felt the rough scratch of his unshaven scruff on her face, reminding her he hadn't stopped to shave. The dark circles under his eyes were a testimony to the sleep he'd lost and the stress he was under.

He cupped her face, didn't hold her tight, just a light grip to remind her he was holding her. Their lips met, and his tongue demanded entrance. Lila's tigress rumbled a purr as a shiver crossed her body. She trembled with a need that couldn't be tempered by her fury.

The birds that had been chirping, even the wind that had been lightly blowing and rustling the leaves paused. It was as if nature had gone silent for her and Cy. Everything was still except for the sound of the rush and the throb she felt in her heart.

She could hear his breathing, the way his pulse matched with hers. Lila's hands rose, creeping up, betraying her, winding around his neck.

Just this once, she promised herself. *Just this kiss so I can feel.* Then she'd let him go, and she'd go her own way.

She lowered her hands, holding his face, tracing the shape of it. She didn't count on his groan when her fingertips grazed his jaw line on the way. She also didn't count on the way it made her react. Her pulse quickened, and her heart tried to beat its way out of her body and closer to his. *What the hell?*

She had to get away from this man. He made her feel too much. She'd wanted to feel, but not this much, not this strongly.

He pulled away, his hands mirroring hers, cupping her face. "Do you really blame me for taking care of you the best way I knew how?"

How the hell could she answer that? When she felt this... this damned thing that was so powerful between them.

"Gavin being in love with you is irrelevant to us. He's like a brother to Vax, and he's sworn to protect you. He would keep you safe from harm. He was the only one I could have put in place to take care of you."

"It's not about Gavin," Lila whispered.

"It's not about not trusting you," Cy whispered back. "You have to forgive me. You have to know why I did that. You do, don't you?"

CHAPTER TWENTY-SEVEN

Cy took Lila's hand in his. He had to get her to understand he would do whatever he could to keep her from harm, even if it meant upsetting her or hurting her feelings.

Lila nodded. "I know." She ran her fingertip over his jaw line, tracing his lower lip. His cock twitched; his body ached to take her. His tiger grumbled at the delay in claiming her.

He picked up the sound of footsteps with his tiger hearing and turned his head.

Vax. He hoped he wouldn't have problems with Lila's brother, but with or without Vax's approval, Cy intended to claim Lila as his. Vax had met them at the entrance to the building, but Cy hadn't been introduced to him yet. He wouldn't have known who he was if Vax hadn't introduced himself inside the building.

Cy took Lila's hand in his and stepped toward Vax.

Vax watched them, his eyes narrow and suspicious, though

he wasn't emitting any scents that gave Cy cause for concern. Vax stopped in front of them, all of them in the shade of the forest. The shadows played on his eyes, making their brilliant blue a shade darker. Or was that anger?

Cy didn't care. He didn't want to disrespect the other shifter, but Lila was his, and he was unwilling to brook any arguments on the matter.

Vax nodded at him. "She's a handful."

Cy inclined his head in a slight nod in return. "That she is." Now what? Where was Vax going with this?

Vax turned to his sister. "I like the way he thinks. He put your safety above jealousy. If you don't see that, you're not the woman I thought you were."

Cy looked at Lila. Her eyes grew shiny as tears threatened. She pushed them back with a slow blink. Her jaw was set. The hand she had in Cy's turned into a firm grip.

She looked up at Cy then faced Vax. "This is between Cy and me."

He watched Vax to see how he would take his sister's response. A slow smile grew on Vax's face, and the handsome tiger shifter's blue eyes turned lighter as his tiger's emotions shone through.

"Like I said, a handful. But what an amazing handful she's turned out to be." Vax leaned close, planting a kiss on his sister's forehead. "I need to get inside. We have a couple of jackals to deal with." With a graceful turn for a man his size, the tiger shifter pivoted and began a purposeful walk toward the building.

"We're coming." Lila pulled on Cy's hand. Then she turned to look at him, a peaceful glow in her emerald eyes. "Are we?"

"We are."

The tiger in him roared in happiness, responding to the emotions it picked up from her tigress. He'd never been one for many words or to show emotions, but this woman, this tigress, brought out a different side of him.

CHAPTER TWENTY-EIGHT

L ila blotted Petra's face with a dampened paper towel. They'd moved the weak tigress away from the cages and the shifters. She lay on a makeshift bed of blankets they'd found in a corner of the large building that doubled as a fighting arena.

The two Rafferty wolves were in a cage, protesting they'd been used, that they'd been blackmailed into the heinous acts they'd been performing.

Lila turned away from the action in that part of the building and concentrated on the pale, weak Petra. She wasn't out for long. She spent more time being fuzzy than unconscious. Luckily, Lila's interception of the tranq had kept her from receiving a strong dosage.

"Cy?" Petra's voice was weak.

"Here." Cy took her hand. "Rest. It's all over."

"We'll get her to Tiero Towers. She can recuperate there. You'll be our guest," Vax told Cy.

Lila held her breath. She knew how she felt about Cy, and

she was pretty sure about how he felt, but they hadn't talked about plans. He had a life elsewhere, she was sure. He was probably eager to get back to that life. What if he had someone, wherever he was from? She hadn't even thought of that. What if she was a momentary diversion and a passing lust that had been built on the adrenaline of looking for his lost sister?

She waited for Cy's answer.

"Can we?" Petra whispered, looking at Cy.

Lila kept her eyes focused on Petra's face, not looking up and across to read Cy's expression. An eternity seemed to pass while Petra's question remained unanswered.

Anticipation built in Lila, along with an unhealthy dose of stress while she waited for Cy's answer. Finally, she couldn't wait any longer. She looked up.

Ebony eyes focused on her face. He had perfectly sculpted lips on a face that was ruggedly handsome. She couldn't get over the fact this man wanted her. Or at least, his tiger wanted her. That wasn't how it was for Lila. It wasn't just her tigress. Was it the same for him? Was it the man *and* the tiger who wanted Lila and her tigress?

"Can we?" Cy's voice was low, as if he waited to hear from her it was okay.

His tongue snaked out, running over his lower lip in a way she was sure he didn't mean to be sexual, but twisted her insides in a good way at the thought of that tongue on her body.

Lila gave him a small nod then cast her eyes away before her scent gave her desire up to not only Cy, but the other thirty shifters in the room.

"I'm going to see what they're doing about her— *our* kidnappers," Lila said.

Cy looked at her then across the room at all the shifters gathered around the caged rangy wolves. She could tell he wanted to go. She could offer to stay and watch Petra, but she really wanted to go, too.

Maia, the leopard shifter, walked up. "I'll watch over Petra if you both want to go. I don't have any interest in hearing anything else those mangy *coyotes* have to say in their defense."

Lila knew she'd hear anyway with her leopard shifter hearing, but was appreciative of the offer. She was going to invite Maia to stay with them at Tiero Towers, where she could heal without being worried about repercussions from any of the Rafferty wolves.

"Thank you." Cy took Lila's hand and headed toward the commotion across the arena.

Vax, Lézare, and the Nielsen twins made room for Lila and Cy.

"What about the jackals?" Lézare asked the Nielsen brothers.

"We'll take care of them, their cousins, sisters, and friends. Any of them who choose to pick the wrong side will be dealt with."

There was finality in the tone of the wolf shifter that made Lila shiver.

Vax shook Reese's hand in thanks. "Why don't you pay us a visit soon? We're having a Council meeting. I'd like to include you if you're interested." He shook Rory's hand next.

The Nielsen twins nodded.

Rory said, "Seems like a good idea. Friends are sometimes better to have around than family, and always better than enemies."

"Come to After Dark. We'll take care of your accommodations. There will be several of us. The Bear Canyon Valley will be sending someone, maybe two. The Arceneaux of New Orleans will have representatives."

Lézare nodded. "True."

Vax continued, "Maybe the Cypress Top tribe will have two panthers in attendance." His jaw tightened. "There may even be a European Tiero, as well." Vax shook their hands.

Lila had no idea any of their European family would be there. Did that mean their father was coming? Or others? Was this about Vax? What was going on?

"We'd be very interested," Reese said. "We'll check our calendars. Right now, though, I'm eager to get some answers and settle a score with my Rafferty cousins." His smile was grim.

"I'm eager to get to my vacation. There's a lovely lady who is patiently waiting for me." Vax looked at Lézare.

"She, Alexa, and Evie are staying busy. I hate to think what they're busy doing," Lézare responded. "She's driving my sisters crazy, wanting to be sure you're okay. I'd advise you to call her."

"As soon as we hit the road, that's a priority." Vax turned to Cy. "Thank you for looking out for my strong-willed sister."

His tone sounded like he was thinking *pain in the butt* when he said *strong-willed*, Lila noted.

Gavin stepped closer to Vax. Lila noticed he wasn't looking at her.

"We found a wounded fox shifter in Dallas. One of the guys is keeping an eye on her to be sure she's not an issue. Any thoughts?"

"That's the shifter I was helping the other night. Remember?" She turned to Cy. "The one the Rafferty wolves were trying to kidnap."

"I remember. She knocked me to the ground in her hurry to get away from the Raffertys."

"We need to help her," Lila told Vax. "She's an innocent in all of this."

"Take care of it," Vax told Gavin.

"Will do." Gavin spun around and left, taking his team with him.

Lézare and his assortment of shifters followed Gavin out the door.

"Keep me posted on this situation?" Vax requested of the Nielsen wolves.

"We'll let you know who's behind it when we get to the bottom of it."

Rory, Reese, and their ten wolf shifters turned toward the cages.

Lila and Cy headed across the concrete floor toward Petra and the leopard shifter Maia. Lila shut out the mournful begging howls the Rafferty wolves were making. She had no interest in hearing how they felt.

CHAPTER TWENTY-NINE

C y pulled into the Tiero Towers parking garage. One of Gavin's men was bringing Lila's car.

The Tiero security team had Petra in a comfortable SUV, stretched out so she could rest. That had seemed like a better idea than having her rough it in his Rover.

The seven-hour drive with Lila had been nothing short of interesting. The Tiero caravan had taken off from the arena, with Vax accompanying Lézare, heading east to Lézare's plantation home to rejoin Callie. Cy and Lila had taken up the tail of the caravan heading northwest to Tiero territory.

The drive had been uneventful. At some point, Lila had fallen asleep. Cy had been unable to tear his eyes from her, watching her sleep. Her full breasts, rounded stomach, the mound of her sex, her thighs, the curve of her brow... There wasn't a part of her body and face he didn't study and memorize while she slept. The long drive had been an exercise in self-restraint. If his baby sister had not been in the SUV in front of them, he would have pulled over and tasted, teased, and ravaged every part of Lila's body.

Instead, he had to temper his cock and his tiger, to keep them on a tight leash while his sexual anticipation reached a new crescendo.

Lila turned toward him as he pulled into the garage, worrying her lip. He didn't want to look away, but if he didn't, she was bound to see the reaction growing in his pants. What the hell had her so concerned, anyway? All had ended well. She was safe, Petra was safe, and justice would be meted out to the Rafferty wolves.

She cocked her head, pointing toward a parking spot. "Take that one. It's next to mine, and it's empty." The way she said it made him wonder again what was on her mind.

"Tell me about it?"

She turned his way, those dark-green eyes of hers mysterious. "Tell you about what?"

"What's eating at you."

She shook her head slightly, as though trying to clear it. "You."

What the hell could be bothering her about him? Was she trying to tell him something? Surely, she wasn't saying she was considering going back to Gavin. His stomach tightened into a knot that felt like it was being pulled by a pair of Clydesdales. He blew a breath out.

"What about me?" Cy barely managed to get the words past the knot that had risen into his chest and was setting up shop in his throat.

"I guess you're leaving." Her voice was flat and emotionless.

"Where do you want me to go?"

Lila gave him a look of disdain, as if she couldn't believe what he'd just said. "Are you serious? You're asking me?"

Cy shut the engine off, turned to face her, and took her hand in his. He ran his thumb along the inside of her palm, up her wrist, and let his fingers rest on her pulse point, feeling its beat, its strength.

"I am. I want to be sure I'm wanted. I don't play. If you want me, you're with me for good. There won't be any breaking up or time-outs or space, or anything. It would be me and you. Forever."

"Fine. Then you're staying here."

The reaction of Cy's tiger drowned out any sound that could have gotten into the car. When his tiger had settled, he finally spoke. "You're on the bossy side, aren't you?" And he loved every bit of bossy, fiery temperament this woman had to give. She reminded him that he was alive. She made him glad to be alive.

She cocked her head at him. "I'm going to show you bossy soon enough."

"I'm looking forward to it."

The elevator ride was a hazy event that Cy would never forget. So was the rest of the next hour.

As soon as the elevator doors closed, Lila grabbed him by the collar and pulled him close. Her nipples were hard, pressing against his shirt, giving him images of touching, licking, kissing, and all sorts of other things he wanted to do to them. Desire slammed into him with a force of an F5 tornado.

He almost didn't recognize the groan coming out of his mouth. "Lock the doors. I want you now."

"I was going to take you up to—"

"Now." Urgency colored his voice with gruffness forged from lust.

Her eyes locked with his. She reached over without looking and fumbled with the keys. He heard a click while he was sliding his hands under the neckline of her peasant blouse, pulling the elastic down her shoulders, leaving her exposed to his fevered gaze.

"Stunning. Fucking stunning. I want you." He traced the lace of her bra, pulling on it with his fingertips, dragging it down closer and closer to the nipple poking out, a hard bud begging to be touched. The scent of her sex wafted upward, infiltrating his senses, taking control of his lust, and pushing it into deeper realms.

Lila pushed closer to him, her breasts against his shirt while she reached behind her back, and, with a deft, practiced move, she flicked the bra loose and shrugged it off her breasts.

Two full mounds with dusky pink tips were there for his pleasure. He cupped their fullness, weighing them while his thumbs pressed into her nipples. He traced a circle around the tight beads, enjoying the way her tips grew harder. She moaned low, her head thrown back slightly.

Lowering his head, Cy closed his mouth over a tip of her breast. Her moan grew louder, driving him to take her by the hips and pull her body firmly to his. Cy's cock pressed against her with an insistence he couldn't deny.

Lila's hands moved with a ferocity that stunned him as she shredded her pants in her fervor to remove them. The fabric yielded as easily as soft butter to a hot knife, parting, neatly rent. She tugged at her top, slicing through the fabric.

While one hand twisted and turned her nipple between his thumb and fingers, Cy's other hand dropped down, over her round tummy to her hip, flaring out in womanly curves. He lowered his hand and moved it toward the center of her belly, just above the waistband of her panties. He made tiny circles above the elastic band, tracing and teasing her flesh. With each passing second, the scent of her arousal grew stronger, permeating every fiber of his being.

He was caught off-guard when Lila twisted out of his grasp, and, suddenly, he was sitting on the thick, plush carpeting of the elevator with his back against the wall.

"You should have used that move when you were fighting the damned jackal Rafferty wolves," he snarled, his timbre deep with passion.

Lila unbuttoned his pants then pulled at his zipper and eased him out with a speed that fueled his need. She straddled him, pressing down on his erection, her moist panties the only barrier keeping him from the target he coveted.

"This move?" She squirmed closer.

"Fuck, no. That move's reserved for me. Alone."

The heat of her sex pressed on his cock, and her eyes were glued to his as she reached down and fingered the center of her panties where her slit was clearly visible, lips wonderfully outlined.

"Your pussy smells delicious. I want to devour it." He couldn't take his eyes off her index finger as it traveled the course of her panties, teasing her slit and her clit. His finger joined hers then replaced hers, moving back and forth gently. He skimmed the satin, allowing the silky fabric to caress her slickness, letting his finger go a little deeper as it pressed toward her entrance.

Lila's body jerked, and she leaned back, her hands behind her, keeping her from falling. He could do this forever, his finger touching her, her body arched, her breasts thrust forward and her nipples dark, tight, and sexy against her full, creamy mounds.

She rocked her hips and pressed her sex against his finger, her body rocking on his hard cock, tucked under her flesh, begging to be in her channel.

With a flick, Lila severed her panties at the juncture of her hips then let the fabric fall away. Cy feasted his eyes on her slickness. Above it, a triangle of trimmed hair shaped like an arrowhead pointed him to her center. As if he needed any help with that.

Lila rose to her knees, moved, adjusted, and then latched her hands on his shoulders, her sex almost touching his cock, and his heart speeded up in reaction. He could feel the heat of her emanating against his dick's sensitive mushroom head. He grew harder, painfully so, his erection straining against the skin that contained it. She pressed down, spearing herself on his cock as he filled her.

Her gasp shot through his body in a burst of adrenaline, testosterone, and an overwhelming emotion he didn't want to put a name to. He gripped her shoulders and pushed her down, his cock's tip now deep inside her. Her gaze darkened as she took him in deeper, her channel flexing around him, tight and slick, a sheath he could be buried in perfectly. He put his hands under her ass and pushed her up then lowered her, the juices from her pussy sliding down his dick, dripping to his balls.

He allowed one hand to go farther behind her, his middle finger touching the soaking, creamy entrance to her cunt while his index finger rested on the rosebud of her ass. He slid his index finger down, coating it with her moisture while he raised and lowered her on his cock, pumping her up and down.

"Touch your clit. Play with it, baby."

She moved her hand between them, trapped in the sweat and sex of them, and put her finger on her clit, then worked it with a maniacal speed.

He slid his index finger upward, generously slick with her pussy's nectar, and placed it on her rosebud with the tiniest bit of pressure. Her cunt tightened around him, as though she was preparing, or nervous. He pushed her up and dropped her back down on his cock while her fingers kept up their insistent, wild dance on her clit.

CHAPTER THIRTY

Lila panted, closing her eyes, caught up in the sensations flowing through her body. She'd had sex before, so she certainly wasn't a stranger to it, but when Cy put his finger on her ass, she clenched and felt her body responding. Nervous and in completely new territory, she started to flick and rub her clit with a ferocity she hoped would drive her trepidation away.

"That's it, baby." Cy's voice was enough to drive her to an orgasm.

The tip of his finger in her ass was sending jolts of pleasure to her clit and making her channel tighten around him even more. She rocked her hips, riding his cock, tilting and angling her body until she was feeling him strike every part of pussy.

Cy raised her up, almost completely off his cock, and his finger slipped deeper into her ass, bringing her confusingly close to climax. Then he dropped her onto his cock, plunging deep into her, impaling her with one long stroke that ripped her breath and a low moan from her mouth, stretching her, pushing her to new heights.

With a fierce growl, Cy pivoted, twisted, and had her on all fours, his cock lined up, her head on her arms, elbows on the floor, ass up. He speared into her with a primal growl then pulled her up, driving his teeth into her neck, right above her shoulder.

She wasn't unfamiliar with this. She knew exactly what he was doing, and she wanted exactly what he was offering. She didn't fight the yell rising to her throat; instead, she let it out as she climaxed, feeling him deep inside her. Wave after wave took her to new levels, each one better than the one before it.

He paused. "Forever?" His voice was gruff with passion... and something else. Something she knew was love.

"Forever," she managed with a growl.

Cy's heat flowed through her as his bite sent a different kind of heat throughout her body.

EPILOGUE

Lila slipped out of her apartment, leaving Cy asleep in bed. She pushed her hair out of her face, pulling it into a loose ponytail because she didn't feel like brushing it.

She and Cy had been here a week. Petra was doing better. She'd been dehydrated, but that was over with, and she'd gained some of her weight back, returning to her curvy state. Lila was going to pick up some food for them. They'd barely left her apartment except for food and to check on Petra.

Petra had Maia and the fox shifter staying with her in her own apartment, a few floors below Lila's.

"Hey."

Lila turned around. She'd been so into her thoughts she hadn't seen her sister Veila come up behind her.

"I don't want to interrupt your time with Cy, but I need some help with the council meeting coming up. I'm stressing it, probably because Vax is. Dad's coming."

"Fuuuck," Lila hissed. "Can't he be talked out of it? I so don't need the fireworks."

"You're not the only one." Veila grimaced, pulling her dress down, adjusting it over her curves. "I need chocolate if I'm going to have to deal with this shit."

"I'm going out for food. I'll pick up extra." Lila hugged her big sister. Maybe they'd both need extra chocolate to deal with the stress of the council meeting.

Veila's nostrils flared. "There. I smell them. New shifters."

"Seriously?" Lila shook her head. She couldn't smell anything.

The door to her apartment opened. Attired in shorts and no shirt, a rumple-haired, sleepy-eyed Cy looked at them. "There are new shifters downstairs. Did anyone else pick up the scent?"

Veila looked at Lila as if to say, *Told you.* "Yes, more choco-late," Veila agreed.

Confused, Cy glanced from one to the other.

Lila wanted to laugh, but something on Veila's face prevented her. "Surely it won't be that bad."

But something inside her told her it would be.

KEEP READING FOR AN EXCERPT FROM THE NEXT *SHIFTERS Forever Worlds.*

EXCERPT

It's a Shifter Council Meeting. This one's being held at After Dark. The city's teeming with shifters. They're supposed to be cordial, but tensions run high when territorial disputes arise.

Curvy tigress Veila has no business falling for Mark Martinez, the alpha of another tribe--a tribe the Tieros have had scuffles with that have lasted several centuries.

Romeo and Juliet's family rivalry had nothing on Veila and Mark's families.

CHAPTER 1

Lion shifter Mark Martinez pushed through the crowd, ignoring the appreciative glances the Dallas ladies were sending in his direction, disregarding the admiring looks at his ass as he passed, not paying heed to the ones who surveyed his package and his wide chest and broad shoulders. He was on a mission. He wasn't here to hunt pussy.

His lion growled, as if to say, "You say that like there's something wrong with pussy."

Yeah, right, as if you ever want pussy anyway. You're waiting for our mate.

His lion growled again, as if there was something wrong with waiting for their mate.

Nope, not a thing. Mark couldn't argue with that. There was nothing wrong with wanting to have the right woman, the only woman, a mate who would be his forever. He'd given up on that, though. Now one thing garnered all his attention. Business. He was only interested in furthering Martinez interests and income.

Right now, Mark Martinez, of the Florida shifter territory, was hellishly pissed at the Tiero shifters of Dallas. They were having a council meeting, their first since they'd moved to this continent, and they weren't inviting the Martinez family.

That was an insult that wouldn't be suffered lightly. He'd rain down his anger on them as soon as their meeting started. His mission was to trespass on the Tiero territory and to violate the sanctity of their precious Towers by barging into their council meeting. He wouldn't mind a peek at Sanctuary, the unique environment created for shifter relaxation and a bit of nature in the middle of Dallas.

The shifter relaxation place evidently wasn't open to Martinez shifters. Mark scoffed at his exclusion from their precious Sanctuary, and sneered. Maybe he'd even have casual, meaningless sex in their damned Sanctuary, just for kicks.

His lion grumbled, though he knew damned well Mark didn't do casual or meaningless sex.

Shut the fuck up. Mark's temper flared. Damn if his lion didn't always call him out on shit.

Wildly enough, the ladies were now looking at him with even more interest, as if the dark side of him was something they'd like to tame. He'd pity them if they saw his dark side; in and out of bed, he could be voracious, insatiable, and rough. Mark kept walking past, his mind on Sanctuary, After Dark, the council meeting, and the Tiero family in general.

He'd heard Sanctuary was a glass and metal bar enclosure that took up the whole forty-third floor of Tiero Tower One. A bevy of caves and tunnels gave visiting shifters space to roam and hide. Above the caves and tunnels, the shifters—in their werecat forms, of course—enjoyed jungle habitat, including oversized boulders.

Tiero Tower One and Tiero Tower Two were side-by-side buildings, built for, owned by, and managed by the Tieros. Five glass-covered walkways connected the buildings, allowing occupants to travel from building to building without venturing outside. The Towers ranked amongst the most extravagant and coveted buildings in Dallas.

Where the hell was his brother? Mark and Mason were supposed to be going to the Tiero Towers together. Mason still hadn't called. Mark took his phone out to make sure he hadn't missed a call.

Nothing.

Was Mason ducking out of this on purpose? Just because his ex was going to be there? This was business. Exes were exes. The two shouldn't intersect; they were at cross-purposes.

Mark forged on. He'd do this without Mason if he had to, though two lion shifters were always better than one when facing a roomful of other shifters who weren't on the friendly side.

Mark shoved the phone back in his pocket and proceeded forward, long strides covering a lot of distance. Blocks away, he could see the tall Tiero Towers, glowing gold as the sun reflected off their windows.

Mark Martinez was always up for a challenge, regardless of the odds.

Let's roll.

CHAPTER 2

I'm going to need more chocolate.

Tigress shifter Veila Tiero grimaced at the thought of her curves and how tight her dress had been before she'd shifted into her tigress form. She was a white tigress, which many of the Tiero tigers were, taking after their father, currently the most notorious tiger shifter in Europe.

She was going to need a lot more chocolate if her father was coming to town. Word had it their father and an uncle or two were flying in from Europe to attend the shifter council meeting her brother Vax—Vittorio—Tiero had called.

Veila got up from her favorite boulder in Sanctuary, stretched, and craved more of the chocolate her half-sister Lila kept them stocked with. She'd have to shift and leave Sanctuary to get some. Since her apartment was out of her favorite chocolate, she'd have to raid Lila's stash. She used to just roam in and out of Lila's apartment without asking permission or knocking—hell, they all did—but Veila couldn't do that anymore. Lila was busy with her new mate, a massive Siberian shifter she'd met while helping out with a territorial matter.

Veila shifted into her human skin and tugged her outfit into place. Shifting was a surefire way to make her clothes look like she'd been playing a sport—or having sex. *Jeez*. Yeah, right. She didn't know how long it had been since the last time she'd had sex. It was too damned hard to find the right man, it seemed.

"You're too picky," her sisters all told her. She laughed that off.

Veila had been sure she and Lila wouldn't be finding mates any time soon. She'd enjoyed the good times they had together. Sure, things were still good, but now she had to share Lila with Cy, her Siberian mate. Veila had to admit he was hunky, just not her type.

She wasn't interested in love right now. She had a career to worry about. She wanted to take over a territory of her own. She had a lot to prove to her father, a man who didn't seem to favor treating his daughters as equals to his sons. She scoffed. She could handle anything any male could.

She slipped out of Sanctuary and down the staircase into After Dark, the club her brother Vax ran.

Partiers from far and wide made After Dark a must-see on their visits to the Dallas. After Dark was known around the country as one of the more high-end nightclubs, rivaling those in Europe. Sanctuary was the largest draw of their customer base at After Dark. All those humans just had to come see the tigers. Though Veila didn't understand the mystique and the draw, she was more than happy to make bank.

Cutting across the club, she had one objective—chocolate,

preferably dark, with a dash of tiny crystalline particles of sea salt.

She took the elevator down to her apartment, passing Lila's on the way. She closed her hearing off, choosing not to let her supersensitive tiger hearing catch any X-rated sounds Lila and Cy might be making.

Her phone vibrating on her hip pulled her up short. It was a text from Vax asking if the executive boardroom was ready. She made a quick U-turn, her stomach in knots. The thought of having their father visit put everyone on edge, but mostly Vax since he had broken Tiero code and taken a human as a mate.

She sighed. She was close to Vax, so if something bothered him, then it bothered her. She fully supported his choice in a mate, and if someone asked, she wouldn't be shy about voicing her opinion. She swallowed the lump in her throat. Voicing her opinion wouldn't bode well for her.

She'd check the boardroom herself because everything needed to be perfect. The Tieros needed the shifter community in America to take this branch as seriously as the European Tiero branch was taken by the European shifters.

Hell, while she was at it, she'd also check on the visiting shifters and make sure their needs were being taken care of. Deep in thought, she walked across the uppermost glass walkway that spanned Tower One and Tower Two.

The visiting shifters were all staying in Tiero Towers Two, all of them in floors below the boardroom, where the shifter council meeting would be held. Tiero Tower One housed the Tiero siblings, as well as Sanctuary and After Dark. Her phone vibrated again. She looked at the screen. *Lila*.

Without a greeting, Veila jumped right in. "Bring chocolate," she told her little sister. "Lots of it. I have a feeling we're going to need it at this meeting."

"Mind if I take a pass? I think you and Vax can handle this. I was going to go with Cy to take Petra back to school and get her situated."

"What? You can't leave me. No. Dad could be coming—" Then Veila got it. "You little witch. You're going because you want to avoid Dad. Aww, come on. That's not fair. You're leaving me, Vax, and Sophie to deal with Dad. That's so messed up."

CHAPTER 3

In the executive boardroom on the top floor of Tiero
Towers Two, Veila stood at the windows, looking out over
the city. The setting sun showcased the beauty of Dallas.
Greenery overflowed in a city that boasted technology
and money.

She turned toward the door when she heard it opening.
Vax closed it behind him. He was alone, his face serious. Veila
wondered if he had the rumor of their father's visit on his
mind. She couldn't let it go. Being sent a continent away from
their domineering father had been just what they'd needed.
Vax had been near a breaking point until their uncles Tito and
Federico had suggested the two move to America and secure
some territory there for the Tiero family.

Having their father so close to them again was bound to
bring up old wounds for Vax. And what hurt Vax, hurt Veila.

"Where's Lila?" Those were the first words out of his
mouth. "And Sophie?"

"Lila's going with Cy to return Petra to Chicago."

125

Cy's sister Petra had spent a month recuperating in the Tiero Towers. She was the victim of a kidnapping and had been destined for a cage fight until she was rescued last month. Now she was ready to go back to college and resume her life.

Vax nodded, as if he wasn't surprised he'd have to fight the battle with one less ally. "And Soph?"

"She's not answering her phone. I'm sure she'll be here." But Veila wasn't really sure at all.

The door opened again.

Lézare Arceneaux held the door open for his sisters, Alexa and Evie. Veila hadn't met either of them, though she'd heard a lot from Callie. She had met Lézare once, in passing, about a week ago. It still flabbergasted her to learn she and Vax had cousins here in America—from their mother's side—that neither she nor Vax had ever known existed.

The most their father had said was to stay away from the New Orleans Arceneaux. She'd never thought to question her father. Then again, she'd never questioned her father, not about anything, and she tried too much to be an ideal child, hoping one day she'd measure up in his eyes, knowing that being a female was an automatic setback.

Her cousin Alexa had dark auburn hair like Veila. She was easy to pick out, based on Callie's description. Callie was particularly close to Alexa. The two spent a lot of time together while Vax and Lézare were talking business. Evie was typically out of town when Callie had been at the Arceneaux home, so Callie hadn't shared much about her with Veila.

Lézare didn't have a chance to close the door before he was followed in by the Bear Canyon Valley shifter, grizzly Jake

TERRITORY

Evans, typically referred to as Doc. Mae Forester had accompanied him to the meeting.

Veila didn't know many shifters who weren't acquainted with Mae. Mae was the widow of grizzly shifter Brad Forester, killed by other shifters many years ago. Mae held the Bear Canyon Valley shifters together, bringing new shifters in, trying to keep her husband's dream for Bear Canyon Valley alive. She was a stunning beauty, though more than a hundred years old in shifter years. Her mate's couple-bond mark had kept her young, and she didn't even look thirty.

Vax had certainly made connections since coming to America. Veila had been so busy with numbers and running her part of After Dark, she'd missed out on meeting these shifters. She looked at her older brother, a glow of pride warming her body. He was the perfect choice to build the Tiero interests here in America.

Mae hugged Veila. "Your brother has said so many good things about you. He's ready to watch you take your own territory."

Veila glanced at Vax, knowing his tiger hearing enabled him to hear what Mae just said.

"Where were you planning to send me?" She softened her question with a smile. She didn't want to leave Vax. He was her best friend the way Lila and Sophie were best friends.

And even though Vax had Callie now, the two of them were still as close as they'd ever been. If anything, Callie augmented the siblings' solid relationship.

A pair of wolf shifters walked in, identical, muscular, with short blond hair. She knew who these two were—Rory and Reese Nielsen, but she didn't know which was which, and wasn't sure she'd be able to tell them apart even after she was introduced to them.

They gave Vax a shoulder hug. One of them leaned closer to his ear. "The Raffertys are taken care of."

Vax cocked his head, a question in his eyes.

"Nuff said," the other Nielsen wolf twin said.

Vax nodded.

The Rafferty shifters were the ones who had kidnapped Petra, and later, Lila. Whatever "taken care of" meant. Veila hoped it was a death sentence.

Wondering if Sophie would make it to the meeting, she checked her phone again for what might have been the thirtieth time to see if her sister had texted. Nothing. Not a word. Was she that busy getting things set up at After Dark?

Veila looked around the room. This should be it as far as out of town shifter attendance went. Oh, hell, except for the rumor her father and two of his brothers would be coming in.

Veila and Vax hadn't told the European Tieros they were having a shifter council meeting, or that they wanted to make it a regular occurrence. The European Tieros—translation: the old-school Tieros—would not have liked that. They didn't like intermingling with other species of shifters, whether as friends or mates. They were totally against taking humans as mates.

Veila wondered how she'd managed to deal with growing up in such a restrictive, close-minded society. She credited her mother with giving her and Vax an easy acceptance of diversity of all kinds. Veila hoped she and Vax had managed to rub off on Lila and Sophie, since they had a different mother. Veila's father had re-mated right after their mother had died.

That union had produced Raphael, usually called Rafe, and two girls, Lila and Sophie.

The shifters all took a seat at the large mahogany table.

"Thank you for coming to what I hope will be the first of many meetings while we all work together to—"

The door opened. Opened was an understatement. Veila flinched at the force with which the door was flung aside.

In the entrance stood a handsome, if arrogant and hard, face, and a broad set of shoulders leading to a wide chest. The chest tapered to a waist that boasted a lot of time in a gym. The striking stranger was a lion shifter; that was evident. Black hair, ebony eyes, a dark tan, and a strong jaw. Veila tried not to stare at the perfectly sculpted set of lips offsetting the hard look on his face.

Something in her stirred. Her tigress. She purred deep within Veila, reacting to the man's lion. *What the hell?* Veila had never been the lion type.

Like you've had any experience with lions or any other shifters, her tigress scoffed at Veila.

Veila bit back an urge to tell her tigress to shut up.

The man locked eyes with her. Suddenly, it was as if no one else was in the room with them, as if no one else was in the world with them. Her breathing slowed, synchronizing with his. The lion's pulse sped up, matching hers.

She couldn't tear her gaze from him. She knew Vax was saying something, but it sounded like distant thunder, indistinguishable and faint.

A second lion shifter joined the first. A brother, she could tell, even if she couldn't see it in their features.

From what Veila understood, everyone who should be here was already seated at the table. And she had no doubt her information was accurate and up-to-date. Vax would have told her if he'd arranged for anyone else to attend.

So who were the two lion shifters? Actually, who was the first one?

A loud gasp tore Veila's attention from the lion shifter.

The gasp came from Lézare's sister, Evie. She stared at the lions, her face having gone ashen. Her eyes were wide and tear-filled.

Veila looked back at the lions. The second lion's face had gone from stoic to concerned to pain-filled, his eyes glued to Evie.

The first lion's grasp on her attention lessened as Veila brought herself back to the situation at hand.

"Was my invitation lost?" Her lion's voice washed over her, leaving gooseflesh behind.

Had she really just thought of him as her lion?

AFTERWORD

Next in the Always After Dark Series: Adversary

Another hot tiger shifter from out of town. Another sassy, bootyli-cious woman. Another sexy story!

Check out ellethorne.com for more of the Shifters Forever Worlds!

There are more than forty shifter stories with their wonderful happily ever afters! And wait until you meet the witches of New Orleans, and the elementals of Colorado, not to mention the polar bears of New York and Russia.

So many shifters! So many love stories! Enjoy!

THE SHIFTERS FOREVER WORLDS

SHIFTERS FOREVER SERIES

Are you ready for it?

I have a whole world full of shifters to share with you. I'm listing them here, in the suggested reading order, though I've tried to make it so that you can pick up anywhere in the series as we all have probably done that at one point or another.

Many of these are organized in box sets for savings. Be sure to visit ellethorne.com to see which box sets are out!

Where's the best place to start? Well, probably with SHIFTERS FOREVER.

SHIFTERS FOREVER starts the series off with grizzly bear shifters and their mates that steam up the pages in these swoon-worthy paranormal romances. From trespassers with hidden agendas to curvaceous women who are ready to take a chance, the stories in this collection will capture your heart.

- PROTECTION
- SEDUCTION
- PERSUASION
- INVITATION
- TEMPTATION
- ATTRACTION

ALWAYS AFTER DARK is a spinoff with the white tiger from Shifters Forever: Vax, born Vittorio Tiero. He's the one that helped Kane out during a shifter battle. Follow the Tiero family, a group of white tiger shifters, as they head to America to find love... and heart-stopping danger. Full of romance, suspense, and gritty drama, this red-hot collection is sure to entertain!

- CONTROVERSY
- TERRITORY
- ADVERSARY
- SANCTUARY

NEVER AFTER DARK is another spinoff that takes place in Europe. Here we visit cities along the Mediterranean and meet the old school Tiero white tiger shifters who are resistant to change.

- FORBIDDEN
- FORSAKEN
- FORGOTTEN
- FOREPLAY

ONLY AFTER DARK takes place in New Orleans. The Arceneaux shifters, led by Lézare, Vax's white tiger cousin—on his mother's side. The Arceneaux are the black sheep of the family. Lézare doesn't cave to public opinion. He dictates policy in the area he rules and he shuns old school European rules and regimes.

- DESIRABLE
- INSATIABLE
- COMBUSTIBLE
- UNDENIABLE

MORE ONLY AFTER DARK takes place in New Orleans. The Arceneaux shifters and the Matthieu witches wreak havoc and find love within this city set on the steamy Louisiana coastline.

- INEVITABLE
- INESCAPABLE

BITTER FALLS FOREVER features Mae Forester's nephew Dane Forester, a freewheeling, sexy, successful, movie star who uses every role and every woman to escape and forget the heartbreak he left in Bitter Falls.

- UNBOUND

BARELY AFTER DARK features more of Mae Forester's nephews! Grizzly bear shifters steam up the pages in these swoon-worthy paranormal romances. From trespassers with hidden agendas to curvaceous women who are ready to take a chance, the stories in this collection will capture your heart.

- CROSS
- LANCE
- JUDGE

EVER AFTER DARK introduces us to the white tigers you learned to love in Always After Dark, Never After Dark, and Only After Dark. See their heritage. Visit Giovanni Tiero and his brothers Federico and Tito. Get reacquainted with Isabel Tiero and meet her sister Capriana Valenti.

- STONEBOUND
- FORMIDABLE

SHIFTERS FOREVER AFTER follows a group of polar bears in New York. Russian and rumored to be mobbed up, they are a powerhouse of shifters, determining the fate of many on the East Coast. Mikhail Romanoff, Layla's father, runs this outfit with an iron fist. Layla's sexy cousin Malachi features prominently in this series.

- COMPLICATION
- FASCINATION
- MOTIVATION

- Captivation
- Flirtation
- Infatuation

Forever After Dark takes place in Denver, Colorado. Enter a world of secrets and forbidden love. Panther shifters who who share their worlds with elementals must decide who they can trust—and who they can't live without.

- Notorious
- Scandalous
- Delicious
- Perilous

UPCOMING SERIES:

Shifters Forever More
Finally After Dark

I do hope you'll be able to join me on this wonderful journey with our Shifters Forever Worlds Shifters and their mates! Hugs, Elle!

To receive exclusive updates from Elle Thorne and to be the

first to get your hands on the next release, please sign up for her mailing list.

Put this in your browser:

www.ellethorne.com/contact

MY PERSONAL GUARANTEE:

THIS WILL ONLY BE USED TO ANNOUNCE NEW RELEASES AND SPECIALS. AND TO GIVE MY WONDERFUL SPECIAL READERS A LITTLE GIFT.

THANK YOU!!!

For sales and news, sign up for the newsletter! Thank you for purchasing and downloading my book. Words can't express what it means to me. If you enjoyed this read, please remember to take a second to leave a review. I'd love to know what your favorite parts were.

Have you fallen for these wonderful characters?

The fun isn't about to stop. Make sure you sign up for the link to the newsletter.

Hearing from you means the world to me. The Shifters Forever Worlds would not be possible without you and your love for reading.

THANK YOU!!!

With much gratitude, I thank you!

ABOUT ELLE

Elle Thorne spent almost as much time denying that she wrote romance as she has writing it. It took her a few years to stop being a closet romantic.

Originally from Europe, she wouldn't dream of living anywhere else but Texas. Unless it was another southern—translation: warm!—state. A southern European by birth, she wants to be near the water and the Mediterranean temperatures if possible.

Where does she like to hang out? Near a lake, a beach, preferably with a latte—extra shot of espresso, please! She's inspired by the everyday men who make dreams come true. She loves a roughneck, especially one with a callous or two on his hands. A man who knows how to fix a car, please a woman, and protect what's his.

Nothing less will do.

ELLE'S NEWSLETTER

To receive exclusive updates from Elle Thorne and to be the first to get your hands on the next release, please sign up for her mailing list.

Put this in your browser:

ellethorne.com/contact

MY PERSONAL GUARANTEE:

THIS WILL ONLY BE USED TO ANNOUNCE NEW RELEASES AND SPECIALS. AND TO GIVE MY WONDERFUL SPECIAL READERS A LITTLE GIFT.

Made in the USA
Monee, IL
10 December 2019